Also by

LLOYD HOLLIS CROOKS

Blood on the Blade

Peeping Through the Keyhole

Ice and Eyes in the Sun: True Love Comes Late, Sometimes

Grenada Ghost

Sister,
Because of You...

A Novel by

LLOYD HOLLIS CROOKS

Patricia Belcon, Ph.D.
Medgar Evers College
Editor

WAYNE BRATHWAITE PUBLISHERS
E-mail: crooksgg519@aol.com
www. lloydholliscrooks.com

Library of Congress Control No. 2018903365
ISBN 0-9666296-9-8
Printed in the United States
Designed by: nkkoprinting@gmail.com

THIS BOOK IS DEDICATED TO

Gloria Albertina Crooks
Merle Cynthia Charles
My loving sisters

I enjoyed this smooth-flowing story/conversation. The comingling of race, current politics, the inclusion of world affairs, personal attacks, and funny anecdotes make SISTER, BECAUSE OF YOU a dynamic reading experience.

Anita Scanterbury

The author did not say it in his narrative, but I am sure the next time the Mediterranean woman and the American woman meet, it will be in bed. A beautiful story, a romantic chaos.

Nigel C.

ACKNOWLEDGMENTS

During writing this book, six people have an input in my text: One from London, England; one from The Republic of Trinidad and Tobago; one from Brooklyn, New York; one from Queens, New York; one from Florida, USA; and one from St. Thomas, U.S. Virgin Islands. I am deeply indebted to them.

Dr. Patricia Belcon, here you are again as my Editor, and, as usual, we chatted about our family, the main institution of socialization, and politics. Seventeen years ago you brought me into your class, and I am still drawing from your bountiful knowledge.

Thank you very much, Dr. Belcon, for your sociological input.

I thank you, Sobek Shu Ankh ("one who returns to the eternal winds"), for your input in my novel, and for informing me of your Indian "tribe." You are a people, NOT a tribe.

Sobek, it was so nice of you and your wife, Khafri Hotep Ba ("one who appears as a peaceful soul"), for inviting me into your beautiful home of love, and for your gracious hospitality. When I said goodbye, you stood, bowed, and said, *Tawahaat Zamal* ("Thank you, brother.") I thank you, too, brother.

Please, Sobek and Khafri, accept my humble respect to you and your people.

Anita Scanterbury, in 1966-67, I worked on your Pitman's shorthand speed-writing skill, and your ability in speed writing improved significantly. Today you are proofreading my text, and I am drawing on your copious knowledge of grammar free of charge. This reciprocity of kindness your deceased Mother, Marion Scanterbury, an institution, described it as, "Two people who cast their bread on the water and got more bread." Thanks one more time, Anita, for letting me have more bread with you.

Fourteen-year-old Brianna Monique Kayla Kiki Crooks, I thank you for travelling from The Republic of Trinidad and Tobago to Tampa, Florida, excited to see me (Grandpa) after being told the last time you saw me you were three months old. I also thank you for entertaining me while I was writing *SISTER, BECAUSE OF YOU* and had no idea of what my text would be while shading from the hot sun in your Father's living room. But I got ideas when you sang "Summertime," *a cappella*. Your voice is a beautiful ribbon of tone ascending to heights that are sensationally operatic.

Kiki, I can visualize your name written in neon lights on Broadway in the not-too-distant future. I love you.

Gordon Charles, in 1984, you were a little boy. Happily you took me sightseeing in the neighborhoods near your home in London; but you stopped suddenly. When I asked for you, you told your Mother, "Uncle Hollis walks too much, walks too far, and I get tired. That's why I'm hiding from him." Gordon, I thanked you then. Today, 34 years later, you are in Generation X, and I am in the Silent Generation. Now I am thanking you again for coming to Brooklyn, New York, to see me, for teaching me how to find bookmarks and other complicated stuffs that I could not understand by the instructions given on the computer.

I thank you, Caleb "BJ" Gibson, for coming at my sudden requests late hours of the nights to help me when paper was stuck in my printer, to help me to retrieve lost documents (being nervous like hell), and to give me the assurance that you will always be there for me (Grandpa) no matter what time of the day or night I call. You reminded me I was your babysitter when your parents were at work, and I also took you to kindergarten school, so coming to help me "is no big deal." Don't let me get emotional, BJ.

And, finally, thanks a million, Lynette Baboolal. Your yeoman, dutiful service as a home health aide and secretary cannot be forgotten. You left St. Thomas, U.S. Virgin Islands, ravaged by Hurricanes Irma and Maria to come and help me. I hope FEMA helps you to repair your house very soon.

Love

Love is not expressed by the hand that wants to paint the lily,
Nature has already painted all the lilies in exquisite colors.
Love is not seen on the thumbs on the ballot box which says,
"Love thy neighbor as thyself;"
Love stays afar from such thumbs for they shout aloud
Their hollow deeds for mammals to hear their boasts:
That's all.
But love truly manifests herself in humans
When we forgive and forget
The hurts other humans unduly afflicted on us.

L.H. Crooks

"Don't copulate with people you don't want to fall in love with,
because indeed you may do just that."

Anthropologist Helen Fisher

My name is Ella Willa Wilcox, not the great American author and poet, Ella Wheeler Wilcox. My Father, James Jules Wilcox, gave me that name because he loved reading Wilcox's work, *Solitude*, which speaks of his life which says, "Laugh, and the world laughs with you; weep, and you weep alone."

I am a black woman, semi-gifted, thirty-five years old, a proud American woman of Caribbean parentage, in the Generation X group, an Independent thinker who votes for the Democratic Party and for the Republican Party only when their policies of social-justice programs are humane.

Proud am I to say I'm exceedingly political. No political party is my favorite buddy. In the Donald Trump and Roy Moore's rantings, Trump said with gusto, MAKE AMERICA GREAT AGAIN. To black me, that's code for MAKE AMERICA WHITE AGAIN. And President Trump proved his true colors when at a crowded meeting in the

White House with lawmakers discussing policy matters, he said loudly, "Why are we having all these people from 'shithole' countries come here." He was referring to people from the fifty-four countries of the Continent of Africa and people of Haiti. "I want people from Norway to come to America." Ninety seven percent of the people in Norway are white. The other white American of Trump's ilk said, without shame, sanitizing slavery, THE FAMILY WAS GREAT EVEN WHEN THEY HAD SLAVERY. Thus, I am akin to the domestic servant, and whoever of those two racist bigots becomes President of the United States of America, I, black Ella Willa Wilcox, will still be akin to the lowly domestic servant if I'm in the employ of Messrs. Trump & Moore, the racist mercenaries.

A man coming from a "shithole" country, named Ghana, who rushed into a burning building to save humans of America, died, Mr. President. People from "shithole" countries are buried in Arlington Cemetery, Mr. President. Did you go to war for America, Mr. President? I can't remember if you did. Tell me, Mr. President. I'm weeping for your vile remarks against my parents and other black and brown people.

I've read, "Don't blame a clown for acting as a clown. Blame ourselves for going to the circus." You are the circus, Mr. President, so I am blaming myself; instead of explaining the hook of my story for my readers to love or criticize my text, I'm talking about "shitholes," instituted by you, Mr. President.

Emperor Trump, you have no clothes on to hide

your racism. And you don't intend to put on any. Oh yes, you have an escape route: Another pathological lie to feed your minions. Mr. President, your less gullible fans should tell you the inhabitants from Norway and the inhabitants from the fifty-four countries in the Continent of Africa and Haiti have the same red-color blood, and "[t]he basic truth of humanity is equality."

It is so nice that I have a job—I may even say I've got a very good job after I graduated from New York University with a Master's degree in Sociology. I graduated the same year of Mr. Donald Trump's racial outburst calling Mexicans rapists, and his Counselor's coining of the phrase "alternative fact," her disguise for a deliberate lie that she uses glibly. Now I use alternative facts to ease my way out of any deceitful, romantic situations with my black-men lovers; and it works. Soon, I may be applying alternative facts on white men whose sole ambition, like some of the black men I once dated, is to sleep with me, then dump me as a piece of rag. I hope in the future I will get a man who sincerely loves me. Thank you, White House Counselor. Your alternative fact is now in my lexicon of tricks to keep fake white men and fake black men out of my clean pants.

I was most surprised when Donald Trump who calls CNN fake news became the President-elect of the United States of America on Tuesday, November 8, 2016. I was shocked like hell when Trump became the President and was told by Bill O'Reilly, the known *Fox Television* journalist, "Putin is a killer." My President replied with certainty, "There are a lot of killers. Do you think our country is so innocent?"

President Donald Trump is paralleling Russia Putin's murderous crime, that of killing political rivals he abhors with America's human rights record. With Trump's lavish un-wisdom of world affairs, I was so sure Hillary Clinton would win the 2016 Presidential election and be the first woman President of the United States to crash the glass ceiling that I bet big on Clinton's victory, and lost. That bad news had me sick, mentally.

I rushed to my doctor to hear if there is also bad news about the health of my beautiful body that I cream daily with my own holistic mixture. My Mother taught me the secret composition of that mixture. My doctor said with his stethoscope all over my body, "Miss Wilcox, you have no signs of any sexually transmitted disease; your pressure is good; your sugar is not too sweet; your cholesterol is fine; your urine has no smell, and it has the right color; your feces, I may say, is not black as you; (both of us chuckled); everything about your body is good as gold. The price of gold is high on the stock market and with President Trump in charge of this great nation the price of gold will soar throughout his presidency."

"Dr. Boatswain, the President should be bigger than a moment."

"I see you don't like him."

"I just wanted to make sure, Dr. Boatswain."

"What do you want to make sure about, Miss Wilcox?"

"I'm confused about everything taking place in

American politics these days. I never thought Donald Trump who grabs women's vaginas and brags about what he does to women would have won eighty percent of Evangelical white women's votes."

"And now that he is your President and mine, what do you think, Miss Wilcox."

I did not answer, but I asked him a question. "Dr. Boatswain what do you think of President Trump who is benign in his views on Russia when there is so much proof of Russia's interference in our 2016 Presidential Election?"

He didn't answer.

"Don't you think the Twenty-fifth Amendment is alive in the White House?"

"I don't know. I am a doctor, not a politician."

I looked him in the eye and asked, "North Korea Leader Kim Jong Un said his Nuclear Button is on his desk at all times. What do you think of President Trump boasting that his Nuclear Button is bigger than Kim Jong Un's, and his (Trump's) Nuclear Button works?"

"Miss Wilcox, they are just bantering."

"Dr. Boatswain, are you telling me that those two crazy fools are having an exchange of light, playful, teasing remarks knowing if any of them presses THAT BUTTON the world would be on fire, and all of us will die?"

"What else could they be doing but playing with words that they can spell?"

"Dr. Boatswain, I felt safer when Mr. Trump said Barack Obama is an illegal immigrant born in Kenya.

Have a nice day, doctor."

I walked out of his office feeling liberated. Liberated from what? Liberated from an educated man who could not see when it is bad for the country President Trump doesn't ever step up, but when it is bad for him (Trump), he steps up with a bull horn. Liberated from my doctor who couldn't remember that Donald J. Trump had tweeted Obama is Psycho. But now that countless people are saying Trump shows signs of being mentally unfit, Trump wants to get rid of the First Amendment which speaks of freedom of speech.

I went to bed thinking whose politics is correct and the pressures on the institutions of Washington because of President Trump.

Next morning, I awoke, stretched, yawned, and looked at my sister, Bianca. She stopped me from uttering any of my overworked complaints. She said, "Ella Willa, don't tell me about the craziness you encountered in your dreams last night. God gave you so many blessings. Do you need a man in your life to share your blessings?"

"Bianca, the man I had in mind, crossed the street, his ears plugged, reading a dirty text on his cell phone, not from me, and a truck killed him. I refused to go to the fool's funeral."

"Ella Willa, why do you make up lying stories? Since you were a child Pappy scolded you countless times for making up those bunkum shits."

"That's true, Bianca. I can give you my deceased lover's name, and the address of the funeral parlor in which his body lies."

"Keep it. You always pick up bums who don't care about you."

It was a clear day in Brooklyn after I shoveled the February 9, 2017, snow with the help of my neighbor, Tweet. Our Father, whom we call Pappy, seventy-three years old, retired, was unable to shovel snow as when he had sinewy arms and with the strength of biblical Sampson. He hates "that white stuff." That's how he calls snow. Once upon a time boys with shovels on their shoulders, eager to earn their own money, sought out landlords from the first drop of snow. I had their snow money hidden under books and other stuffs on the bedroom table. I knew the front-door bell would soon be ringing. The bedroom table was always cluttered because it was the easiest place to put all my stuffs. Unlike me, Bianca put everything in order on the bedroom shelves: receipts on shelf one, magazines on shelf two, and incidentals on shelf X. When we lived together as teenagers I had asked, "Bianca, what is on shelf X?"

"Ella Willa, I don't ask you what is on the cluttered bedroom table that is for your books and mine. There is no space for my things, not even for the ribbons for my hair. I hope when you leave Pappy's house, get a house of your own, and get a decent man, you'd become a tidy woman; and you will not put your thongs with your knives and forks in the same drawer."

I have not changed. I still hide my money between books on the cluttered table and throw down everything else in the closet in the basement. When the boys came for their snow money I knew where to find it. Bianca stays with her friends sometimes and when she comes to visit me at Pappy's house, she knows where to find my hidden money. I have no safe with code numbers; and I have no secret hole in my mattress to hide money. Bianca always loses the house keys. She knows that I hide the house keys outside under a stone in the flower garden. She collects them. She goes to my cluttered table, moves things around, and finds my money. She always tells me it is a loan, but her loans are never paid or repaid. Then she calls.

"Hello, Ella Willa. I love you. I dropped by Pappy's house this morning to borrow some money."

"Bianca, after you found the money on my cluttered table, did you arrange the things on my cluttered table as neatly as the things on your shelf X?"

"No; I was too busy. I hadn't the time."

I am five years her senior. From childhood, we laughed riotously, and when she told me, "No; I was too busy," I rushed out of my office choking with laughter, and the girls asked, "Bianca came for money hidden on your cluttered table?" They, in turn, related stories about their siblings who never repaid their debts.

At the water cooler, the girls spoke about what we did last night, the dinners we cooked for our families, children's school grades, and the price of sending their children to college. We stayed away from politics, but Juliet said, "I WAS WITH HER (Hillary)." And Hazel answered, "But she lost to Trump who will lock her up now that he's in power." But Hilda changed the topic and asked the question, "Ella Willa, when are you going to get married and have children to join the mothers' bunch at the water cooler?"

"My sister wants me to marry a white man and have bi-racial children, so I dreamt of doing it in bed with your husband, Phillip."

"My white husband?" Hilda asked, her eyes popping out of her head.

"Yes, girl. You want to know all the poses he made me do in my dream?"

"No! No! No!"

"Hilda, I'm so sorry you don't want to know how Phillip enjoyed it."

All the girls laughed straight into lunch time, Hilda too.

I tell the girls the month and year I was born, but I never tell them the day. I never want to be surprised with a gift from the one-door-ninety-nine-cent store for the second time. But I give expensive gifts to my work-mates, not to show off, but to see their smiles. People's smiles brighten my day, and so does my sister's. I love her dearly.

Bianca and I live with Pappy. Our Mother, Enid, is dead. Pappy said he would disown us if we ever marry a white man. Bianca always tells Pappy, "Race has no color," and she'd move out one day after her eighteenth birthday. She told me why.

"Ella Willa, you are a chicken. You are afraid of Pappy. I can no longer live by his Eighteenth-Century rules. He still thinks we are teenagers and can tell us whom to marry. He still thinks I'm his baby who needs a change of pampers. He asks any boy who drops by to see me and talks about homework what is his intention. I was glad when Bobby told him, 'Old man, my good intention is to buy you a pair of binoculars to see what Bianca and I do on your bed when you are out of town.'"

"Did you tell Bobby to apologize to Pappy?"

"He did. But Pappy would not stop interrogating my friends. Ella Willa, Pappy is a good man, a good Father, a good provider who has taken care of us since our Mother died. I will kiss him and tell him goodbye tonight. But I want you to be there as his little poodle sitting next to him when I tell him goodbye."

I was there, and her goodbye to him did not surprise him; did not annoy him; nor did he shed a tear. He surprised her and me.

He calls her Little Girl. "Little Girl, you know where I keep my check book. Get it for me." She brought it; he wrote her a check with a large sum but did not sign it. He kissed her goodbye and walked to his bedroom smiling.

She shouted: "Thank you, Pappy. I will use the money to travel to London to marry a white man." She looked at the check. "Pappy, you did not sign the check."

"When you show me the white man's photograph and your plane ticket, I will sign the check."

I did not ask her when she's leaving for London because I knew she's not going anywhere soon. All I thought was if Bianca leaves, I only would have to share Pappy's inquisitiveness, his self-serving politics, and his old-fashioned way in his 3-bedroom house. That thought had me fearful of the future.

Then I questioned myself: If Bianca does move out what would I tell Pappy if he wants me to move into Bianca's room which is next to his. I wanted to ask her advice but refrained. I did not want her to see I'm really a chicken, so I looked for another way that I should address Pappy. I know he likes to play scrabble, and he likes to use big words.

I prepared breakfast. He was born in The Republic of Trinidad and Tobago (inhabitants are nicknamed Trinis). He is now a Naturalized American, and he likes when I surprise him with a Trini's breakfast like what his wife gave him: Coffee whitened with milk and sugar, flat bread (Trinis call bake), crushed salted fish in scrambled eggs, lettuce, and a small glass of orange juice. The first words he'd say after he belched, "I wonder what my lazy daughter who did not sleep home last night had for breakfast this morning?"

"Pappy, Bianca is an American woman, born in Brooklyn Hospital, on De Kalb Avenue, and I'm sure she's at McDonald's right this minute with her girlfriend, Shelly-Ann, who doesn't cook."

"Shelly-Ann doesn't have a stove in her apartment?"

"Of course, she has a stove; but she doesn't cook."

"Do men marry women who do not cook?"

"Of course. This is not the time when you were born. Pappy, can you find your Alcock's English Grammar book?" I purposely changed the subject.

"My head teacher, Mr. Best, made us study that book from cover to cover. I'm a syntax expert."

"Joanna Napoli told me her Father used that book too in Jamaica. She also told him she wanted to leave home but. . ."

He stopped me. "Don't you want to leave me, too, Ella Willa?"

Oh how I hate to hear him call my name and look at me with his suspicious eyes. "Pappy, I've got to dress for work. The next train would be packed like sardines in a tin if I did not get the 8.05 at Newkirk."

"Why not finish with what's on your mind?"

"What's on my mind?"

"The day you are going to leave me alone in this big house in Brooklyn."

I did not answer

"BD, thanks for this Caribbean breakfast." BD means Big Daughter, and Pappy calls me BD when he wants to extract information from me.

I looked at him.

"What I like about your sister is that she tells me what is on her mind. You behave as if you are afraid of me."

"Thanks for our lovely conversation, Pappy." I left the table.

I caught the 8.05 as the train pulled in Newkirk

to reach to work on time. I work at Little & Brathwaite Think Tank, a nonprofit company, as a research clerk. I took out my yellow pad, and I read my research paper I had prepared for my job assignment as the train snaked its way downtown Brooklyn. Midday I stood under Skylight which is on the second floor of the old Williamsburgh Bank Building at One Hanson Place, Brooklyn. My stomach was growling, and I rushed to buy takeout at either Halal Kitchen, Denny's Chicken Wing Kitchen, or Cesar's Tacos Kitchen. The policewoman, four feet, three inches, hungrier than I, rushed after me, and I told her to go ahead. She said, "Sister, you save my life. I had a tough morning with Flatbush rowdies."

Another voice is heard. "Sister, can you save my life, too?"

"Who are you calling me sister?"

"I'm sorry for my silly introduction. My name is William Baxter. I do not have a New York ID, but I can show you my British passport for you to see I didn't give you a false name."

"Go ahead. You don't have to give me your biography to jump the line."

"For your kindness, may I buy you lunch?"

Before I could answer, he asked, "From which truck?"

I looked in his eyes.

"Please, please."

"From Halal Kitchen."

"We have a lot of Halal kitchens in East Ham, London."

"My sister, Bianca, lives in East Ham."

"You visit Bianca often?" We found seats.

"I visited her twice in the five years that she has been there."

"What's your name?"

"Ella Willa Wilcox."

"Miss Wilcox, I'm extending an invitation to you to visit me when next you come to London. I will pick you up at the airport and take you to Bianca."

"Thank you, William. I know you are a hungry Englishman in downtown Brooklyn, but I wouldn't know who you are even if I meet you in London with five British passports."

"Please, take a chance on me, Ella Willa." His smile was captivating.

"Okay."

"Last year I was in Manhattan, and I went to the Comedy Club. Have you gone to see standups there?"

"I do standups every morning with Pappy so I don't have to go there."

"Who's that?"

"My Father."

"How?"

"When I'm preparing Pappy's breakfast, he always asks, 'Ella Willa, when are you going to get married and leave me? And I hope it is not to a white man because I will disown you.'"

I reply, "Pappy, I will leave your house when you write me as big a check as you wrote for Bianca when she was going to London. And, Pappy, if a white man loves me you will know before I put your eggs on the table."

He takes a sip of his coffee; he looks at me, and says, "Ella Willa, I hope it is not the man in the moon."

"Pappy, I never knew that guy is white." He cracked up with laughter, but I knew his anti-White sentiment he acquired working on Wall Street as a legal secretary is real. He tells me of those white, upstart, young lawyers whose respect is only for their computers.

I stopped talking of the conversations Pappy and I had, smiled, and looked William.

He smiled too. "How often do you practice your standups with Pappy?"

"William Baxter, I even practice in my sleep what I will tell Pappy in the morning."

"That means you are already practicing how to tell Pappy you are leaving home without letting your conscience cry for your ingratitude to him?"

"Something like that."

William and I got off sitting on the concrete edge at Atlantic Station, and we walked to the corner of Schermerhorn Street and Third Avenue. He read aloud KHALIL GIBRAN INTERNAL ACADEMY HIGH SCHOOL. "I've read Gibran's works. Have you, Ella Willa?"

"Yes."

We ended our stroll on Fulton Street. His observation was keen. "I notice the majority of the people walking by are Colored people."

"I prefer you say Black people."

"I notice White people are not seen on this street."

"They live closer to the Atlantic Ocean."

"You do standups on Fulton Street too?" He expected me to smile. I didn't.

"White people are coming back to black Brooklyn because of economics."

"I like your one-liners."

I pretended I did not hear him and stretched my hand. "William, my lunch time is over, and I'm not returning to work. I have to leave you now. Next week I will be going to New Orleans to visit my childhood friend, Dr. Joanna Napoli, and I will tell her I met a gentleman from London named William Baxter."

"Don't forget to tell Dr. Napoli I paid for your lunch, and you had to rush home and leave me because of Pappy's curfew."

We laughed heartily. He went into his wallet. "Here's my card if ever you come to London. I will be traveling to Atlanta to do a bit of business, and the following day I will be on a flight back to London." He shook my hand and said, "Can I hear what you will tell your Pappy about white me?"

"Pappy, I met William Baxter, a decent white man who does not live on the moon, and he invited me to his home when I visit Bianca in London."

"What you think he'd say?"

"A limey! A cockney lay-about! You will be going to his home? Are you afraid he may hijack you?"

We laughed aloud, and ran into the subway. He

went uptown. I went downtown. But before boarding the No. 2 train to Newkirk, I called Bianca in London and told her everything what William and I talked about.

2

I live on Rogers Avenue, a one-way street where traffic goes north. I saw no vehicle driving north and was thinking of William but a car reversed south on me to get a parking space and knocked the thought of William out of me. The words that came out of my mouth were nasty. "William Baxter, I hope the next time we meet I will not be using such words." I opened my gate, closed it, walked up the steps and opened the door. I stepped in softly, went to my room, and all my belongings were neatly packed away. My bed was made up with clean sheets. I wondered if Pappy cleaned up after me to encourage me not to leave him. Then I changed that thought. Probably Bianca called Pappy and told him that I saw a white man, and he should approve of my friendship with that white man. My body had an urgent call because I do not use public bathrooms, so I answered that urgent call.

After answering that call, I knocked and opened the door. "Pappy, every time I reach our gate I have to run inside."

"Why, Ella Willa?"

"Because I have to use the ladies' room to answer a call."

"Then I will move the house to wherever you are so you can answer all your bathroom calls without running."

"Thank you, Pappy."

"You see how much I love my BD."

That was a nice introduction to tell my racial-minded Father who hates any idea of miscegenation to the bottom of his heart about William Baxter. But how to begin my short thesis was my problem. Nonetheless, I went into my handbag and took out notes that I had written when I met William. I began: "Pappy, I was sitting at Atlantic Avenue subway station, and I learned some history about Fort Greene today when I read what was written on a flat stone. Let me read it to you, Pappy: 'After George Washington evacuated his army to Manhattan in 1776, the British imprisoned captured patriots aboard eleven decrepit ships in Wallabout Bay, adjacent to the present British Navy Yard Industrial Park. The horrific conditions in these makeshift prisons cost the lives of 11,500 patriots. Their remains are buried in Fort Greene Park, which was named after Revolutionary War General Nathaniel Greene. Their crypt rests below a majestic Doric column designed by Stanford White and dedicated in 1908.'" I looked at him and smiled amicably.

"You, Bianca, and I have strolled around that signpost quite often in the past. I can tell you the exact spot where that stone billboard is. What perked your interest to read to me today what is written on that stone?"

"A tourist."

"You were her Fort Greene guide?"

"The tourist's name is William Baxter."

"From Africa?"

"From London."

"Bianca's friend?"

"I don't think so. I told him when I'm in London I'll call him. I gave him my e-mail address. Pappy, I'm going to prepare your dinner."

After a silent dinner he said, "Ella Willa, this morning you left our conversation hanging as a fox's tail; tonight you do the same."

Bianca's advice came to mind: Ella Willa, don't let Pappy con you as when we were children. You are a woman now. Always cut him off. Leave the dinner table with a sweet smile.

"Good night, Pappy." I showed him my sweet smile. I closed my bedroom door, and said softly, "Tomorrow is another day, Lord. I hope Pappy gets a woman to get off my back. How long would I be having this load? "

Tomorrow came.

At the water cooler Agnes said, "Ella Willa, how was your weekend?"

"I met a tourist from London, and he asked me to check his IQ."

"What was the test you gave him?"

"I told him to tell me a bit of the history written on the stone billboard at Atlantic Avenue. I saw him reading it over and over as if he's going to have a civic test in class."

"He passed the test?"

"With flying colors, Agnes."

"This Londoner couldn't find anybody but you to ask for a voluntary quiz?"

"You know strange things happen in downtown Brooklyn."

"Like what, Ella Willa?"

"Agnes, I saw a man, without shame, on the sidewalk begging for money to buy weed, and people were putting money in his cup. I also saw a woman changing her panty a hand-length away from a policeman."

"What the policeman did?"

"He pretended he did not see her, and he walked a distance farther east."

"By the way, you finished your research paper for Robert?" Robert is the boss.

"Robert did not seem to be pleased with my research paper. He said it has a bias slant, and I was not objective. I spent two days studying the ethnic rivalry in Brooklyn between Caribbean Blacks and American Blacks in the fifties. I quoted Dr. Eric Williams, one of the foremost research scholars in the world. Williams said when the colonial masters left the Caribbean the natives were already in training to assume governmental duties and the natives were educated and were fit and eager to take over from the British expatriates. In the United States, the white slave masters never taught their slaves to read, and slaves were punished if they were caught with a book. What makes me f--kin mad is when I hear Caribbean blabber mouths saying things as, 'Dem American black people are lazy. They're only waiting on Welfare.' If they read the statistics of who gets the most Welfare, they'd know black Americans get the least Welfare. The ignorant Caribbean sour mouths don't know, or refuse to know, the suffering American blacks went through, and dem f---kin Caribbean ignoramus are now enjoying the fruits of Black Americans' toils and sacrifices."

"Isn't your Father and Mother from Trinidad and Tobago, and that country is in the Caribbean?"

"Yes. But they, at least, know a little American history because they read my and Bianca's civic homework and absorb the knowledge of what they read about American history."

My day was over at my job. But on my way home my thoughts went on what I'd told Bianca when she was seventeen years old. "Bianca, you are destined to fail high school. Your life is only about boys."

"Ella Willa, I will graduate and go to college. Do you want to bet?"

She did graduate from Brooklyn College and moved to London with a fat check from Pappy. I am still living with Pappy and abiding by all his ancient rules.

As I opened the door, Pappy said, "Ella Willa, you got an e-mail."

"How could you know that? You don't know my password."

"The Russians didn't know Hillary Clinton's, but the hackers passed it to a certain source."

"Who is your source?"

"Me."

I was very annoyed thinking Pappy had a hacker's knowledge, unknown to me; he hacked my e-mailed, and he had read my e-mail. I refused to go on the computer. I went to the kitchen and prepared egg-plant and pasta for dinner knowing fully well he'd hate that dinner. While preparing dinner I could hear Bianca's voice in my ear saying, "It's time to leave Pappy. Aren't you tired of his plentiful bullshit lectures of morality with his little kindness platter."

Pappy and I sat at the table. I was fulling my mouth every second and mixing my food as mud knowing he hated when his children ate that way. He was looking at me with his fork hitting his glass. When Bianca and I were teenagers, we knew when he kept hitting his empty glass with his spoon he was mad with us about something. She didn't care, and never cared, but I cared. He never beat us but he tortured us, sorry, only me. My plate was empty; I forced out a belch, and said, "What remains will be our tomorrow's dinner." He looked at me. I expected him to burst out with the weight on his thoughts with his full plate, untouched, before him but I blocked him. "I enjoyed my dinner. Excuse me, Pappy. I'm going to put my dirty plate and cutlery in the dish washer."

"You can wash my untouched dish too, Ella Willa Wilcox." I could feel his anger. "You purposely cooked that stuff because you are annoyed with me about something. Your Mother did the same when she was annoyed with me. Before she died, did she tell you the best way to hurt me without cursing me, was to cook that Italian-pasta stuff?"

"Why are you so ethnocentric? You believe your Trini foods with all that starch are the best tasting food on the planet."

"I was a good husband to your Mother. Wasn't I?"

I did not answer that question. "I'm going to check my e-mail." As I said that, he dipped deeply into his dinner. I felt sorry for him because I realized he was very hungry, and I should not repay him in the way my Mother did when she did not get him to acquiesce to her unreasonable demands.

I turned on my computer. At a glance I saw three letters: one from Bianca, one from William, and one from James. I opted to read the one from James because I didn't know who the hell James is! The letter began: "My dear Ella Willa Wilcox, it behooves me to know our allied friendship has a way of showing a double face. Moving into the eastern bedroom that Bianca once occupied wasn't the topic you wanted to delve into but you used it to piggy back the question of your wanting to leave your nosy Pappy."

Immediately I knew James was Pappy.

He continued:

"I met someone in the strangest of places that I'm beginning to like—not love. Her love partner is also deceased. Both of us do not believe in premarital sex even at our advanced ages—she is seventy; I am seventy three. The tail will not be wagging the dog if I ask: Can she overnight in the bedroom next to me, and she will leave the next morning after spending the greater part of the night chatting with me? I will talk about the virtues of my deceased wife, and she will talk about her deceased husband."

I stopped, made a cup of tea, and returned to James's e-mail.

"Ella Willa, please, don't use your overworked euphemisms to reply by stating the ball is in my court. I don't play tennis, but my best hobby was kite flying with razors on the kites' tails in Fyzabad. I always cut down the competition. All my competitors booed me off the stage in Talent Search when I lost my pitch to the octave of the song, *Fools' Paradise*. In Fyzabad parlance, they shouted at me, "Chook (pick) him down wid (with) ah (a) gullet as if you chooking cocoa off a tree. He's no f---kin good. That was a sad day in my life because the prize was ten dollars, and I wanted that money to buy a new outfit and bees wax to slick my hair like Nat King Cole's."

I stopped, sipped my tea, and laughed my ass out imagining what courage he mustered to get off that stage, and how his flat face, and sloping head would have looked had he won the competition and had money and had bought beeswax and slicked his hair like Nat King

Cole's.

I was laughing and reading. "Ella Willa, you can call your adviser/sister to frame your best answer because she, like her Mother, Enid, doesn't call a spade a shovel. You know the dirty adjectives she'll put before spade (smile). I love you. James."

His e-mail ended.

Emotional was I to know Pappy is asking me for permission to bring a woman into his house that he sacrificed to buy with the small salary he got when he worked at Chase Manhattan Bank in the sixties. I hurried off the computer. I did not read another e-mail, not even the one from William as much as I wanted to hear from him and obsess his male smell. As I walked by the standing mirror in the hallway I could see my countenance glowing. Pappy pretended he didn't see my happy face, but said, "BD, the taste of this delicious Italian pasta on my palate is divine."

"Pappy, that is what happens when you stay long to eat. Hunger becomes the mistress of your stomach that takes away your choice and gives you hers."

I smiled my way to the tub and thought of the day Bianca and I played in the bubbles. That thought left me. "Oh my god! I did not read Bianca and William's letters. How come both of them e-mailed me the same day?" I pulled a towel off the rack and dried my body. I always admire my body. Let me say, worship my body. When worshipping my body, I think of the day when I will give my body to the man I love—not to abuse it, but to cherish it as his own. Sometimes I spend my spare time looking at pornography, and I like what I see. I never used to look at that stuff but Bianca introduced me to *On Demand* Pornography when Pappy was sleeping. She would say, "Ella Willa, I like when a man does that to me. What about you, Miss Saint?" I never answered her question, but I wished a lover did that to me too.

I dried my body, went back on the computer, read Bianca's e-mail, and loved what William said in the first line of his letter: Each night I dream of you. When are you coming? I smiled. My thoughts changed to the high snow outside when I heard the noises of my neighbors' shovels outside making bass sounds on the pavements. I put on my heavy coat, sweat pants, and boots, and joined the neighbors. Tweet, my favorite neighbor, and I chatted and shoveled in rhythm. We laughed about the habits of our aging parents. Then we threw salt on the pavement in front of our houses, and said goodnight.

3

At work in the Power Room at One Hanson Place, of the ten research employees, Randolph, Atiba, Helen, and I did not discuss our research papers that were late for presentation, but we had everyone joining in our 2016 American Presidential election discussion initiated by Helen.

"Bernie Sanders wants to take money from the rich and give that money to whom?" Helen Zico continued. "After Bernie shares all the rich people's money to the poor, and the poor people spend all the money given to them from the rich man's coffers, everybody will become poor, and where do we go from here?"

"Bernie never said that!" Atiba shouted.

"He said something like that," Helen shouted louder.

"Something like that is not the same thing!" Atiba stamped the floor.

Randolph said, "Let's have a vote from the group of those who voted for Hillary and those who voted for Bernie in the primary."

The vote was even.

I had a ready-made answer. "That is why the Trump man won. He had an even amount of vaginas to grab without condemnation from the Evangelical ministers."

Laughter resounded in the Power Room.

In my lunch time I went on my laptop and wrote my return e-mail to Pappy: "My dear James Jules Wilcox, tonight your dinner will be steak with thick, brown gravy; white rice; black beans; red beans; mixed veggies without broccoli which you hate; a lofty salad; and soursop juice, home-made by me.

"Now I can tell you, Mr. Wilcox, without hiding that I have already obtained a return ticket for London on British Airways. I will be traveling in two weeks to London to see Bianca after I visit Joanna Napoli in New Orleans.

"Of course, your friend—you have not told me her name—can come and sleepover for many nights as she wishes, and she does not have to leave 'fo-day morning, as your wife would say in her heavy Trini accent. It would be somewhat precipitous for the preservation of my rights if I say your friend should not come by you or make love to you.

"In London I will be seeing a white guy named William—and I know how you feel about white people. But our relations will be platonic.

"In William's e-mail, he gave me his address and phone numbers, and I will be giving them to you to apprise you of my whereabouts. I will be living with Bianca, my adviser (smile), and she has some of your critical ways, though converse to yours sometimes. Probably I will be jumping from your frying pan into her fire because she will be emphasizing in my thick skull love has no color.

"Before I leave, I hope I will meet your friend, bond as sensible women, and I will be able to give Bianca the good news about the women who will be in your bed. I also hope before I leave you will tell me titbits of your life story for I believe it is an interesting story, but hidden from your children. Oh yes! You told Bianca and me the story of a young woman who did not know you, and you did not know her. She was crying. You asked her why was she crying. She said she has to go to Harlem for a free medical test to see if she has HIV, and she needs a partner to go with her because she hasn't the courage to go alone. She asked you to go with her to the clinic and take the HIV test too with her, and you did. Both of you became good friends. I'd asked you, Pappy, what was the result of the test; and you told me it was negative. That was a noble act, Pappy. If I didn't have HIV I would not have gone to the clinic with her. She would have had to find courage with another John Public on the street. Not me.

"I have to cut this letter short because I'm going into the Power Room to discuss my research papers. Some of us are extreme left; some of us are extreme right. Some think President Trump is plural because Tuesday Trump is diametrically different from Thursday Trump.

"I love you, Pappy. Ella Willa."

I hit *send*.

Then I told myself I forgot to ask Pappy what is his woman friend's name.

The Power Room had a character of its own. On the walls were large photos of Malcolm X, Martin Luther King Jr., Colin Kaepernick, Jessie Jackson, Barack Obama, Eric Williams, John Lewis, Paul Robeson, Marcus Garvey, Pele, Oprah Winfrey, Mayor Bill de Blasio, and many other political figures and community leaders. There were also very large, painted pins on the wall that read: #ME-TOO; TIME'S UP; MY BODY, MY CHOICE; AM A WOMAN RECLAIMING MY TIME; BLACK LIVES MATTER TOO.

Aziza Baxtin began. "Is turnabout in politics fair? Yes, it is. The Republicans when they were in the Opposition did everything in their power to block Obama's proposals when he was the President. I hope the coward Democrats do the same now that they are the Opposition and the Republicans have the White House.

"I am from the Deep South, and my great, great, great grandfather was hung on a tree by a white mob. I am not going to pussyfoot and shade what is in my mind: Any black man who takes a white woman to be his wife should be OSTRACIZED by black people. She emphasized the word Ostracized. The same goes for the black woman who has a white man in her bed."

Baxtin was booed. "Racist! Who are you to tell people how to live?"

Emil Psaki was the moderator. "Let her continue.

You will get your chance to speak and to say why she is right or wrong based on your subjective judgment."

There were salvoes of nasty brickbats that went on and on till the end of the working day. But my mind was saying: "Ella Willa, you are happily going to London to see a white man, probably to fall in love with him, and if your Father's feelings are akin to Aziza Baxtin's, that's your Father's feelings, don't let it be yours."

The work day ended; I subwayed home; and prepared dinner.

While Pappy and I were having dinner I said, looking into his eyes, when he had no food in his mouth, "Pappy, if that woman who will be coming to sleep in your bed has children who marry out of their race into the white race, what would you tell her in a civil conversation?"

"I paid an expert to investigate her background three generation back."

"To find out what?"

"What I want to know."

"The DNA experts say nearly all the people in the world have different races in their blood."

My mind left Pappy and me at the dinner table and went on the time Aziza and I had gone to Jimmy's Bar. When I was drunk, and she was drunker, I told her that I am going to London to mix my coffee with milk.

"Ella Willa, why not let his f--kin milk mix with milk of his kind; and let your light coffee mix with blacker coffee?"

"That's no fun. I want a new kind of fun. Mixing that

coffee with milk—I can imagine what it would be. Good!"

"You'll really let a white man on your belly?"

"Other places, too. And I hope you will not ostracize me from your friendship if I have a white lover."

"I hate you. Let's go home. You did not critique me in the Power Room. Why, Ella Willa? I hope when we exchange theses you will see all my reasons why I think the way I do."

"I'm looking forward with baited breath to read why you won't stop hating white people. My Father hates white people too, but not as deeply as you."

Still at the dinner table and for the first time I felt comfortable talking to Pappy without finding reasons to leave. I felt like Bianca and treated Pappy as my equal. "Pappy, my friend Aziza's views are worse than yours."

"What's it?"

"She hates white people with a deeper passion than yours because her great, great, great grandfather was hung on a tree by a white mob."

"Let's change the subject. When are you leaving to be in William's arms?" He smiled.

My smile was broader. "In two days. Haven't you been counting the days to know when that mystery woman will be moving in after I'm gone?"

He laughed aloud. "Have you checked your e-mail?"

"I'll do that after my loving Father and his first born dine in style." I kissed his cheek and left the table. I did not tell him I'd already read the mail from him. He checks his mail sometimes a month late.

The day before I leave for London would be his seventy-fourth birthday. I did not know what to buy for him. I called Bianca and she advised, "Buy Pappy sexy underpants so if his Phantom woman is young she will have an appetite." She laughed vulgarly.

"Bianca, Pappy has never shown me signs before of wanting to have a new woman in his life because he is forever talking about our Mother."

"He has shown me."

"How?"

"You are too close to him to see anything that is different in his then-and-now character. If that woman comes before you leave, encourage him to try companionate marriage. Let her stay in the bedroom next to Pappy, and you should use the back step to come and go. You should leave early in the mornings, and come home late at nights so the mystery woman would have to prepare all Pappy's meals. Ella Willa, don't let Pappy outlive you. I need money to graduate for my Ph.D., and I live too far away to come and search your treasury on that clogged table." We laughed boisterously.

"Ella Willa, what's all that joke about?" Pappy asked.

"My adviser was talking to me. She says she will call you tomorrow." I hung up.

The next day an e-mail came from William. My heart was pounding. His letter read: "I recited the Fort Greene inscription on the stone in front of the mirror with only one mistake. I did not say, 'Ella Willa Wilcox, I love you.' When are you coming? I hope you will be in London before I leave for Germany. My firm got a big contract in Germany, and I will be there for two months. When I come from Germany I will recite the words on that Fort Greene stone and tell my mirror because of that stone I met you. Gibran's works are all over my house for you to read if you come by me. I will take you and Bianca to see all over London as tourists do. How is Pappy? Give him my regards.

"Waiting with all my love for you,
William, the white man (smile)."

4

It was the day before I traveled to London. I let Aziza proofread my research paper, and I turned it in to Dr. Basrat Pouchi who supervised our research that day. I added to the excerpts I took from Dr. Eric Williams' *Capitalism and Slavery* there is no difference between the Caribbean black man and the American black man because both can be shot with a white bullet, and the summation from the *status quo* before investigation will be, "There's probably a valid reason why they were shot."

My other similarity between the two men in my thesis is both were descendants from the Continent of Africa, dropped in different ports from the slave ships.

I had dated a black Caribbean man and a black American man; one sex was good, the other was heavenly. I did not need Wikipedia to give my *carte blanche* observation. I laughed my ass out thinking of the difference between my Caribbean-asinine lover and my American-almost-perfect gentleman. Their guile was different; their ghosting was a gulf apart; their good looks were the same. Their cultural difference that shocked me most was: The American took me to white restaurants "to dine;" the Caribbeanite took me to Caribbean restaurants "to eat good food." Those were the predicates they used. My sociology brain lit up whenever they used those predicates in their invitation.

I asked Caribbean Westy, "Is Westy your legal name?"

"Ella Willa, my friends call me Westy."

"Is Westy your first name or surname?"

"Neither."

"If I take you home to meet my Father, that's the name you'll give him?"

"Why not!"

"If the police write you up for speeding, what name you'd give him?"

"You are trying to find out what is my real name? Are you a detective?"

I knew I was not taking this fool home to meet my Father so I did not mind meeting him and documenting his foolishness for posterity.

I asked Westy, "Why do you say let's go and get good food to eat?"

"What's wrong with that?"

I did not know he'd question my question so I had to fill in my thinking time with my best smile. "Nothing really. What happens sometimes is that I'm not used to your West Indian accent."

"Ella Willa, I'm not West Indian! I'm Caribbean."

"Sorry."

He took me to Banana Boat, a very nice Caribbean restaurant, in Flatbush, Brooklyn. On the wall is a picture of Mayor de Blasio and a man, probably the owner, or an employee, close to each other. When he ordered the food, he asked the cashier, "After the Mayor took that picture, did he sit and eat the good food here before he ran for election?"

She said, "Mister, are you a food detective or you come to buy food from us to eat?"

I told Westy, "Let's sit, and when we see the menu we will decide if we will take home the menu or eat it here." I did not want to sit and eat because I know his habits. Just as I do not know the day I would die, I know if we sit and eat he will agitate the cashier to find out if the Mayor sat and ate in the restaurant.

"Ella Willa, I'm going to the bathroom."

"Westy, when you come out of the bathroom, please, walk to my table. Do not go looking for the owner or any-one to find out if Mayor de Blasio ate here."

"I am a West Indian man."

"I thought you are not West Indian but Caribbean?"

He did not answer my question.

"You, American women, like to govern your men. Not me!"

"Mr. West Indian-Caribbean man, all I'm telling you is: If you come out of that bathroom and go and question the cashier or any employee if the Mayor sat and ate in

Banana Boat, I will leave the restaurant, and you. Permanently!"

He came out of the bathroom and asked the cashier, "Who is in charge here?"

"Why?" she asked.

I did not wait to hear more of Westy's agitation. He once told me agitation is finding out the truth. I have gone out with him before, and I know he was going to start a battle. Wherever he goes, he starts a battle. I walked out of Banana Boat, with my appetite watering for the dishes in the glass cages. I enjoyed the two years of our friendship but I was tired of my back bending to hold our friendship.

My mind went on the past. "Westy, let's go to hear Tony Bennet at Barclays Center."

"He can't sing. Let's hear Banju Banton next week at Madison Square Garden."

"Westy, let's go and hear Patti Austin in a centennial celebration of the First Lady of Song, Ella Fitzgerald, at Brooklyn College auditorium."

"That white woman can't sing like Ella. She wants to make money in a black neighborhood. That's all. You are a fake like that woman."

"Which woman—Ella or Patti?" He did not answer. "Westy, you took me to Paradise Hall to hear calypsonian and reggae performers belching all those nasty songs about women. And what was worse was to see your Caribbean women dancing and singing happily those nasty calypso and reggae songs about them and their bodies. I saw the way that Caribbean woman was gyrating her body to the floor. That woman has no class."

"That's culture, fool. She has more class than you. And she is a nurse."

"You mean a nurse's aide. Most of those Caribbean nurses' aides wear nurses' uniforms and pretend they are RNs."

"How do you know?"

"I know. I'm a sociologist, and I make it my business to study behaviors."

That argument went on for hours. I admitted when I was wrong with my ethnocentric rantings, apologized for the stupid things I said about Caribbean women, told him my parents are from Trinidad and Tobago, and I should be ashamed of the way I characterized Caribbean women as if the behavior of one is the behavior of all. He would not admit when he was wrong. His theme was, "I's a born Jamaican."

Whenever I meet my girlfriend, Georgia, a native of Jamaica, living in New York for twenty five years, she greets me, "Watch you mout, I's a born Jamaican. Not from Jamaica, Queens. I's from Jamaica, Jamaica."

To stop me from laughing, she'd say, "Ella Willa, wasn't Westy a donkey ass?"

Then I will begin my laughter afresh.

The two years I spent with Westy as his lover, I never invited him to my house. We were as strays copulating in half clean motels. The turbulence never ended, and we sometimes used that turbulence in bed as an aphrodisiac.

He knew his performance in bed always made me change my mind about leaving him. Countless times I wanted to change my mind and end my relationship with him but I could not find the last straw until he insisted in finding out if Mayor Bill de Blasio sat down in Banana Boat and had a meal with the "homies," the participants who sit, eat, and speak about "down home."

It did not take me long to be befriended by Lou, a Southerner, living in New York. He and I caught the No. 5 Flatbush train at Newkirk every morning. It seemed we left home the same time to catch the same train. We sat in the same car next to each other in small-bucket seats made to fit Japanese women's bottoms comfortably. We never smiled or say a word to each other. We got off at Bowling Green station. He walked down Water Street to Goldman Sachs building. I walked to 125 Broad Street, one block away from his building. Our travelling together every morning without saying a word to each other lasted for a month, less or more. I rushed into the train one morning and held the door for him before the door closed on his toes.

"Thank you very much. You prevented me from being late for work today, and today is a day that I shouldn't reach late. I'm Lou."

"You are welcome. I'm Ella Willa."

"For a month or so we have been two silent strap hangers afraid to speak American English because we thought one, or both of us, can't speak the language."

"Seems that way, Lou. Let me break the ice and offer you a free ticket to hear Billy Taylor at Carnegie Hall. I'm inviting you to accompany me to hear Billy Taylor if you do not have a prior engagement."

"I love Billy Taylor. He taught me at Jazz Mobile in Harlem when I was trying to improve my skill as a pianist. I have one of his compositions, and I am working on it to play it for him one day."

"Lou, you haven't said if you want the ticket."

"Of course. That would be my birthday present."

"When is your birthday?"

"Today."

I handed him the ticket and sang a line of *Happy Birthday to you.*

"When is the show?"

"Tomorrow. Is my invitation too late?"

"I can go because I do not have to find an excuse for my Mother to help her that day."

"So you are a Mama's boy?"

"Not really; but on Saturdays I usually drive her to and from the supermarket."

"I hope I will have a son to help me when I get old."

"How far away you are from having your first born?"

"At my last physical, Dr. Boatswain did not find a fetus."

"Who should have put it there?"

"You are good."

"I like jazz."

"Your improv equals Billy Taylor's? I listen to Billy Taylor too."

We laughed as old friends.

"Today is Friday. Would you like us to travel together?"

"Sure. Where can I pick you up?"

"At Pappy's."

"Is that an address?"

I smiled. "Here is my card with my address."

"So this is where your Pappy lives?"

"For the past fifty years. Dress up?"

"Please, no. Nobody dresses up again."

"What time should I be at Pappy's gate?"

"Five."

It was a cool summer. I did not overdress but I took a light jacket and my deceased Mother's words of advice: "Ella Willa, whenever a man takes you out, you must walk with 'vexed money.'" The first time she gave her girls that advice, I asked, "Mama, what kind of money is that?" She said that is your own money that you should keep in your bra in case both of you get vexed with each other because he may want sex as payment for taking you out; and if you don't want to give him sex, and if he refuses to bring you home, you will have money in your bra to pay for your transport home.

I did not put vexed money in my bra. In a modern woman's world, I walked with my Chase Debit Card in my pocket book. Lou pulled up at 5.01 pm. He came out, opened the door for me, and said, "Ella Willa, you look lovely."

"Thank you, Lou. My eyes are telling me the weekday crowd on the subway hides your good looks. Over which bridge are we going?"

"Which bridge is better at this time?"

"Manhattan."

"I will follow your guidance."

"Today?"

"Always, if you allow me."

"What about the other person?"

"She is with me in the car."

"Your math counting is horrible."

"No such thing. Goldman Sachs hired me for my math."

"Little & Brathwaite Think Tank hired me because I am able to research you."

"What else do you research?"

"Whom should a black woman trust with her heart—a black Caribbean man or a black American man?"

He looked shocked at my question.

"Let's talk about Billy Taylor tickling those black and white keys instead."

"I'm so sorry you change the subject."

"Next week I will invite you to the Power Room of the Think Tank when we are discussing all types of crazy subjects."

"I'd love that. Can't wait for your invitation."

He drove in the parking lot on Seventh Avenue, came out, opened the door for me, and a valet took the car. I wanted to kiss him on his cheek and say thank you, but I told myself that I'd wait until he dropped me home at Pappy's gate. Then I had another thought: Pappy had asked me before I left home if it is the first time I'm going out with Lou. I said yes. Another thought flashed before me: If Pappy sees me kissing Lou, he'd criticize my over friendliness with a man that I know only a day. Then Bianca came to mind: Ella Willa, why are you so afraid of Pappy? Then my final decision was: I will tell Lou to drive over the Brooklyn Bridge, and I know a place where Westy always parked with me. There I will kiss Lou deep and make love to him for his birthday.

Billy Taylor opened with *Summertime* followed by *Somewhere Over the Rainbow*. He played nonstop for one hour, and he ended with *All Of Me*.

The applause was thunderous. He returned and played *Misty*.

"Ella Willa, isn't he a great pianist?"

"Yes, he is. But Pappy says Art Tatum is the best; and Tatum's playing inspired pianist Vladimir Horowitz and conductor Leopold Stokowski."

"Your Father plays piano."

"Just a little."

"Where did he learn?"

"In Trinidad and Tobago."

"He plays a lot of calypso?"

"No."

"How come?"

"When he was a boy, his classical music teacher never let her students play calypso music."

"And your Father became a man, and he is still obeying his music teacher's nonsense?"

"He told me he never showed interest in calypso from childhood. He dropped his classical music, and he loves jazz music with a passion."

"Besides Tatum, who else is his music idol?"

"I'll tell you that if we have another date."

Lou drove out parking and said, "Why don't we go somewhere and dine."

"Only if I pick up the tab."

"Why?"

"Yesterday was your birthday so I want to extend it."

"Ella Wheeler Wilcox, I read of her at Tufts. How come you change your middle name?"

"Pappy did not know how to spell it."

"Pappy gave you money to spend on me tonight?"

"No. I'm using vexed money from Chase to pay for your birthday dinner."

"Is that Donald Trump's new kind of money? With it, you can buy Ivanka Trumps's clothes made in China."

I told him what vexed money is.

"So you are treating me with Chase's vexed money tonight. What about next week, and the following weeks?"

"If you behave as a gentleman tonight I'd know what kinda money to put in my bra in the future."

"It is so nice meeting you, Ella Willa Wilcox, the sociologist."

"Nice meeting you, Lou, the mathematician, at corporate Goldman Sachs that pays their employees half million for bonus. When next I have to take out the vexed money from my bra to dine you, I will tell you." His smile met mine.

I was silently falling in love with him. I can take him home. Pappy will like him.

We had a wonderful dinner. He gave the tip. I thought it was too much and wondered if that was his way of saying Ella Willa I have money too. But he read my mind and said, "I worked as a waiter when I was in college, and welcomed tips from customers."

At my gate, I kissed him on his lips. I wanted him to pull me in and kiss me deep, but he didn't.

"Good night. See you on No 5."

"Goodnight. See you on the No. 5 on Monday, Lou."

Pappy was propped in his big chair with two pillows. "You had a good time, Ella Willa?"

"Billy Taylor was great."

"Did he play anything from Errol Garner's *Concert by the Sea*?"

I began singing *Misty*, moved to the piano, he sang the full song, and I accompanied him. "Pappy, you refused to go when I invited you to hear pianist John Lewis at Brooklyn College. I guess you are saving your energy and romance for when I leave for London."

"I hope that Londoner is not a Cockney lay-about."

We laughed.

I went to bed a happy woman and kept thinking: Lou is so different from Westy. It was Sunday but I could not wait for Monday to board the No. 5 train at Newkirk. But I knew Pappy will make a comment.

"Ella Willa, this Sunday dinner is delicious, delicious! You must have had a romantic Friday, before and after cheering Billy Taylor?" He displayed his cunning smile. "Do you want me to tell you about the first delicious dinner your Mother cooked for me before marriage?"

"Naughty, you used to go in her apartment before marriage? Let me put Bianca on the phone to listen to your premarital romance."

"Sure. Put your counselor on speaker."

"Sorry. I forget London is six hours ahead, and she's sleeping."

I went to bed thinking about Pappy's way of getting me to talk about my dates; but my greater thought was about Lou's slow and romantic style. I liked it. I felt sorry that in two days I will not be seeing him. He gave me his cell number, but I did not give him mine. We traveled together up to Wednesday. We chatted from Newkirk to our stop at Bowling Green. We went to Bowling Green Park every evening, looked at Ellis Island, and spoke of the history of immigrants who passed through Ellis Island. We looked at boats taking tourists to the Statue of Liberty. Knowing Wednesday would be the last time we'd be together, as the sun kept sinking I made it easier for him to hold me in his arms. We kissed each other countless times. Eight o'clock we were still leaning on the rails that prevented us from falling into the bay.

"It's time to go home and pack, Ella Willa."

"You want me to leave because I'm not attractive to you."

"No. Because Pappy is waiting to close your suitcase."

"How do you know that?"

"To prove what I say, I will hold your hand at Pappy's gate until he calls you inside."

We stayed an hour longer romancing each other oblivious of our surroundings.

He walked me to the gate. Looked me in my eyes and said, "Good bye, Ella Willa. Don't lose my cell number. Remember there'll be no more No. 5 trains for now. But I hope there'll be many more in the future." He did not look back.

"I hope so, Lou. Goodbye."

Immediately my mind ran on William, and soon I'll be seeing him in London.

5

British Airways landed on time at Heathrow Airport. Bianca helped me with my suitcase and led me out. As I bent to put my suitcase into the trunk of a car, a hand helped me. It was a white hand. I shouted without looking around, "William! William! William!"

"Yes, Ella Willa, the woman I met at Atlantic Avenue, Brooklyn." He hugged me; I kissed him, stepped away from him, and looked at him and as if I found a million dollars.

"William, you and Bianca tricked me. Where did you know her?"

"Ask her."

"She never told me about you. She's no good."

"She's my best friend. We have been in touch by way of technology. Get in the car next to me."

"I'm not going to get in the car unless you tell me how long you and Bianca have been plotting to get me to come to London."

"That's our secret."

William started the car and drove slowly. I walked just as slowly and said I am not getting into the car. William stopped the car, and Bianca got out. I spoke in Bianca's ear and said softly, "Sister, because of you..."

"What?" she asked.

"I'll tell you when we get home." I got into the front seat, and William drove us to Bianca's apartment. Bianca prepared dinner. We laughed and talked endlessly.

"Little sister and big sister, let me recite the wordings on the standing stone at the foot of Hanson Place in Fort Greene, Brooklyn, where I met Ella Willa."

When he reached [t]he horrific conditions in these makeshift prisons cost the lives of 11,500 patriots, Bianca stopped him. She remembered reading the writing on that stone how the British imprisoned captured patriots and their inhumane treatment to them. I was about to applaud. She looked at me, and I folded my palms.

"Bianca, why did you stop me?" William asked.

"I didn't want to be reminded of your British soldiers' cruelty to us."

He didn't continue with his recitation. He said, "Here's my number in Germany. Call me. I will be there on business."

He kissed Bianca on her cheek, and I walked him to his car. I did not wait for him to kiss me. I kissed him deep. He dropped himself into his mini Cooper convertible and drove off.

A new day met Bianca and me speaking nonstop.

She told me of her grades at London University. I told her of my research papers about American black men and Caribbean black men that generated heated discussions that I enjoyed to the hilt. Jillian told me she loves Caribbean men. Kai told me Caribbean men are too sneaky, and all of them have more than one woman in their lives. I was the adjudicator between those two girls.

"Ella Willa, why didn't you research Stop and Frisk by New York Policemen?"

"That will be my other research topic when I return." Bianca looked at me quizzically. She was about to say something but stopped.

"How is Pappy?"

"I took your advice that he should have a woman to keep his company, but the woman never came for me to know her."

"She probably has an ax to grind."

"I hope not."

"Why do you let Pappy have such a hold on you? You are no longer a child. You are a woman. Ella Willa, tell me the truth: When last you had a romance—not with Sociology textbooks—but with a man?"

"Yesterday."

"Don't lie to me, girl."

"I'm talking the gospel."

"You are like Pappy. You don't like church, so leave out the word gospel. What's his name?"

"Lou."

"Which hotel he took you?"

"Bowling Green Park."

"In the grass you had sex?"

"Lou and I walked holding hands, and then we sat on a bench and looked at the Statue of Liberty until it was late. I wore a low cut blouse, and both of my breasts were rubbing on his chest."

"You are still using that old trick to see if your date is not gay."

"Yes; I'm still using it."

"Was the act consummated in the park? Mine was at eighteen."

"No; but I felt good with his deep kisses. And because of you forcing me to come to London, I'm not with him consummating the act in a motel."

"What became of you and Westy?"

"When I left him, he mailed a book to my job, and he autographed it: 'You, dumb American Bitch, read F. Donnie Forde's *Images of America...CARIBBEAN AMERICANS IN NEY YORK CITY 1895-1975*.' The book speaks of, among many other historical settings, the 'second wave of West Indian immigration which began about 1900 and continued right up to the Great Depression.' That book also speaks of Caribbean people's arrival and record the story of how they design their new lives in the Big Apple. That book is Pappy's atheist Bible."

"You can use as your Bible that oldie style of letting your breasts rub on William when he comes from Germany. But, please, brush up on that 1800s breasts-exposed style by using your imagination as a vulgar woman in bed. I can tell you what my English girlfriends and I do to know if our dates are gay men or men with live gristles for hot women."

"Tell me! Tell me!"

"It's time to sleep. I'll tell you another time."

"How do you get around?"

"On public transport. Stay home and sleep. Do not unpack all of your things. You will not find your passport. I've hidden it. You will not be going back on the day written on your passport. Call Lou and tell him you will not be coming to finish the act."

"Bianca, because of you...." She did not let me finish the sentence.

"Because of me you will be marrying William Baxter. Call your Pappy and tell him Mr. Baxter is English white, love has no color, and he should bury his hatchet of hating white people." She closed the door and left.

I rummaged through my purse that night. I emptied it. I did not find my passport. I threw out everything in all my bags. So Bianca meant what she said, I mumbled. Jet lag sent me to sleep.

The next day I did not know when Bianca came home and cooked a sumptuous meal. She woke me up, and I ate as a pig. "Bianca, I'm ready to hear what you do in a romance to know if your date is gay."

"Williams comes back in a week so I have time to tell you."

"Have you tried the men's manhood technique?"

"Here we call it the hard balls technique. I've left

Pappy five years ago. Before I left Brooklyn I had great times." She paused, looked at me, and said, "I enjoy clean sex with risks. I could not enjoy life without sex. Life without sex is no life."

"You are telling me Pappy was preventing me from having sex, and I can find a man in so many different places, even in a laundromat. To quote Gail King, Oprah's friend, 'at my age, I want a man who already has a washing machine,' so I will not be looking for a man in a laundromat, period! Thank you, Gail King."

"Did you bring sexy, sleeping clothes? Night time with music will bring out your woman's charm. When William comes I will be putting you out to go and try companionate marriage for a year. Then after a year both of you will call Pappy and tell him that you'll are coming home as husband and wife."

"Ha! Ha! Ha!"

"I'll be going to make a speech at a Hospital Labor Union to talk about Brexit and Donald Trump's ban on Muslims coming to the United States, and I want you to help me with a paper about America's 2016 Presidential Election."

"Return my passport, and I'll help you." I realized she meant not to give me my passport so I stopped asking for it.

"Ella Willa, did Pappy accompany you to the airport?"

"I prevented him from coming."

"How did you win that battle?"

"I was determined that he should not come because I knew he would have been too emotional."

"Did Lou call you?"

"He gave me his number, but I did not give him mine."

"Why?"

"Knowing that I'm coming to meet William, and I will be living in his house, and Lou will be calling me at odd hours, I did not give him my number. I can't handle a long-distance romance with an on-the-spot romance happening at the same time. I tried it once, and it did not end well. You and William planned hiding my passport?"

"Sister, because of your blinding worship for Pappy I am protecting your sanity. It is time for Pappy to get a woman to keep him warm. When our Mother died there were times when Pappy was like an uncircumcised Philistine. I wish I were like David with my slingshot to shoot out his cruelty to us, which he called keeping us in check. He bitched about everything you did. He knew I was not going to stand his shit so he left me alone. He told me I was a leper. And you remember what I told him."

"Let us not rehash that."

"William returns tomorrow. Be ready for him."

"Please, help me."

"Pack your things because I will be putting you out."

"You are sending me to live with a man that I know nothing about."

"I had my people to run a check on him. My computer ran a check on him. And my womanhood ran a check on him to see if he wants me too."

"What you found?"

"I slept in his house one night, and he treated me as his little sister. He is clean. He smokes a little pot at home only and never with friends. Socially, he doesn't take more than two glasses of wine. He is a successful car salesman with his own dealership."

"Would I have to look for a job for survival because you hid my passport, and I can't return to my job in Brooklyn?"

"No."

"How do you know?" I walked to the kitchen. It is spacious with every gadget one can think of. "Bianca, let me cook today."

"Ella Willa, today is the last day I will let you cook for us. Let me remind you William comes tomorrow, and I will be putting you out."

"I thought you were making a joke."

"I'm not like Pappy locking you in. I'm locking you out to see the world."

"For the sharks to eat me."

"When you go back to Lou in Brooklyn, you'd have experience."

"Because of you, he'd not be waiting for me." I dished out food for both of us.

"I'm glad you know that. You have to let down your bucket here in London. I like what you cook. You are a good cook. Remember how you used to feed me when I was little." She looked at me; I could see her gratitude.

"Let's eat and talk, girl."

"Bianca, you have not taken into account that I've lived thirty five years in Brooklyn and conscripting me now as a soldier to fight urban-guerilla warfare with a white man who probably doesn't know much about a black woman's likes and dislikes could be dangerous to me."

"What gives you the feeling that William never had a black woman?" She looked at me. "I have been here for many years by myself, and all the bumps and bruises I encountered in London made me strong. You have me and William to protect you."

"I only know William for a short time and in a casual way sitting on a street bench. I will not be comfortable if left alone with him." I kept eating but I was looking at my little sister. When we were children I did everything for her. I spoiled her because I loved her very much. She was always ahead of what to say to Pappy if we disobeyed his rule. One of his rules was to shower before nine at nights and to be in bed nine thirty.

"Ella Willa, did you follow my night rule?" Pappy asked.

"Yes, Pappy. I showered at nine."

"Bianca, what time did you shower?"

"Pappy, you removed the clock from where it is supposed to be, so I could not see the time to know when it is nine."

"So you are going to bed without showering?"

"I am still looking for the clock to know if it is nine.

Pappy, where did you put the clock?"

"Where it is supposed to be."

"I did not see it. But if you say it is already nine, I'll have my bath right now."

"Were you watching *Roots*, Bianca?"

"The TV is on where it is supposed to be so I had to watch what is taking place in Africa."

"What is taking place in Africa, Bianca?"

"A black man named Koonty Koonty who resembles you is saying he is no slave."

Pappy could not stop laughing. He told her to have her shower. What surprised me, and Bianca more, was he kissed her when she came out of the shower. He saw the look on my face, and he kissed me too on my both cheeks. I couldn't remember him kissing us as children. From that night I knew how a woman feels when she is kissed tenderly. I also knew my sister could invent a lie in a nanosecond. I can't. Nonetheless, I wanted to hear of her love life.

"Bianca, are you ready to tell me about the handsome men you have dated?"

"None was handsome. I don't care for handsome men. I like a man with nice-body parts. I remember him if he has a square jaw, thick lips which I like very much, black and white hair, things like that. Any color, any race, any religion, is okay with me."

"Tell me about the Welch."

"I did not understand him and most times I gave him the wrong answer to his questions so it was easy to part company with him."

"What about the Cockney?"

"I did not understand Bick too, but I liked him. We broke up after a year of dating. I told him that I was pregnant."

"Bianca, I'm sure both of you were happy with the baby news."

She looked at me. "He said, 'You say you are pregnant. That's fine with you, not with me.'"

"What do you mean, Bick?"

"You could have prevented it. I am a chemist. I could have liquidated that black bastard.'"

We were on the Abbey Road. He is a little man with red hair. I picked his wallet. I stopped my car, opened the door, pulled him out, and told him, "Mudder fukker, find the footprints of the Beatles when they walked on Abbey Road." I emptied his wallet and threw it outside.

I felt sorry for the way Bianca treated Bick, leaving him far away from home, and with an empty wallet. "Bianca, what you did with his baby?"

"I wasn't having any baby. I wanted to test how deep was his fukkin insincerity."

I left the other two men's plight with Bianca for another day. One was Caribbean born, the other was from Mauritius. I put the wares in the dish washer and thought of what Pappy told me: "That sister of yours will make her husband bend on his knees if he tries any shit with her."

"How do you know that, Pappy?"

"The way she's not afraid of my punishment I can't see her obeying any man. She would not be afraid to poison a man if he hurts her feelings."

"You and our Mother never taught us to be unkind or to poison anyone. You led us to the fountain of truth, kindness, and forgiveness."

"Your sister is that kicking horse your Mother and I led to that fountain but she refused to drink. She only kicked."

My memories were rekindled to another time when Bianca kicked. Before moving to Flatbush, we lived in Bedford Stuyvesant, a black neighborhood, and were bussed out to Bensonhurst, an Italian/Irish white neighborhood, to school. There was a girl bully who thought Bianca needed a lesson in knowing who controlled the commuters on the bus. Bianca was respectful to the driver. She always chatted with him before she chose her seat next to me in the middle of the bus. I always sat by the window; Bianca sat in the aisle. Wilma purposely bounced Bianca's leg when she walked to the back of the bus. Then again she purposely bounced Bianca's leg harder when she walked to the front of the bus to chat with one of her buddies. Wilma's main intention was to start a fight with Bianca knowing she, Wilma, is bigger in stature than Bianca. That was Wilma's Waterloo.

Bianca got up. With lightning speed she held the rail on bus; she kicked Wilma to the ground; and dropped on her as a dead log. Wilma, in pain, crawled to the back of the bus that evening. But for the rest of the school term she sat in the front seat next to the driver to guard her safety.

My flashbacks ended. I began to prepare my mind about how I should greet William, and what should I tell him when he returns from Germany. Bianca told me to call William Bill. How should I greet Bill when Bianca put me out and where would I sleep: In the same bedroom with him or in another bedroom far away?

Bill had told Bianca that I would sleep upstairs on the king-sized bed in the master bedroom of his massive house in the Holland Park neighborhood and he would sleep downstairs because he would not like to disturb his Brooklyn guest because of his nocturnal habits: He walks from bow to stern in his house thinking of what he'd do tomorrow; what he'll tell his customers; what would be the market and the economy. He'd sip wine; he'd be in and out of the fridge emptying ice trays because he likes to crunch ice with his strong, white teeth.

"What are you thinking of, Ella Willa?"

"Bill will be coming home tomorrow, and you'll be putting me out."

"Do you want Pappy's Seventeenth Century words of advice or mine?"

"Pappy is in Brooklyn with his woman so I want yours."

"Mine is simple—very simple."

"I'm listening."

"The first three nights sleep upstairs. In London, people dress to have breakfast, so be dressed for breakfast. But when he calls you for breakfast thank him for the wonderful time you are getting. In London people will make a long story about why the rain did not fall on any given morning. For my Master's degree three professors took me to lunch, and I was warned by my friend, Betty, to be prepared to talk nonstop about everything that is not important but be humorous. Tell Bill about Pappy when he was fourteen and he went on the show Scouting for Talent in Fyzabad, Trinidad and Tobago. You know the story, so imitate Pappy's heavy Trini accent that he applies when he was giving us the joke.

"On the fourth night, find your way next to him on that twin-sized bed downstairs wearing the clothes I bought for you."

"That's a small bed."

"He'll have no space to hide from you."

"And?"

"You took care of me when I was a tot and made the wise choice of creaming my body with Vaseline instead of one of those high-priced-Madison-Avenue products that gave me bumps. So you can think of what Lou or Westy would do to your breasts or if you prefer what Bill will do to your whole body. Take it from me these English boys will romance your body first. And you'd like it."

"Does that mean I have to take care of Bill's body?"

"If you prefer, let him take care of you, and do not go upstairs to sleep on that king-sized bed."

We laughed aloud as when we were kids and Pappy gave us time to look at *Roots*. We went to bed.

Tomorrow came. It was now today.

"Ella Willa, Bill will be here in an hour, and I do not like what you are wearing. Change it."

It was summer. I went into my drawers and chose a silk bra, a transparent top, and grey shorts. I must have creamed my body for an hour, not with Vaseline, but with a product Bianca used on herself. My hands were tired, and I fell asleep with the jar of cream on the floor. All I felt were somebody's lips on mine. Then that somebody was not there when I opened my eyes.

The noise from merriment in the living room awoke me. Bianca and Bill were chatting aloud like school children when school was over. I walked in the room.

"Ella Willa, how was your sleep?" Bill asked.

"I dreamt someone kissed me on my lips when I was in heaven."

"How many times Saint Peter kissed you?"

"Once."

"I can do magic and make Saint Peter kiss you twice."

Bianca spoke. "When Ella Willa and I were very, very small, not after the age of five, Pappy used to do that to know if we were really sleeping, and we used to snore aloud as if we were sleeping for the past two hours."

I spoke. "And stupid I used to open my eyes, and he'd ask, 'Did both of you say your prayers?' I'd answer and say, No, Pappy. And I will pull Bianca off the bed to say our prayers. I did not lie to him because I was afraid he'd punish me."

Bianca said, "Bill, I don't know why Ella Willa was

so afraid of Pappy. I hope she's not afraid of you. While she was sleeping I put all her luggage in your car. She is ready to leave. Ella Willa, did you like the way Saint Peter kissed you?"

"It could have been better, Bianca."

"When you are in his big house you can teach him the better way."

Bianca walked me down to his countryman Cooper and whispered in my ear, "Don't bring geography into your relationship. You are a big girl now."

I smiled, slipped into the Cooper, and rehearsed all Bianca's teachings of how to let him hold on to me. He gave me an hour tour of London before he took me home to his mansion.

6

"Bill, this house is lovely."

"Ella Willa, it is not this house, it is our house."

"When did you put my name on the deed?"

He smiled.

"If I have to stay upstairs at nights alone, I am going back by my sister."

"Nobody will be tying you with rope to the bed post upstairs."

"Thanks for letting me know before it gets dark."

"Thanks for leaving Brooklyn and coming to London to see Bianca." He paused. I looked at him sternly. He smiled, "And me."

"What do you and Bianca plan to do with me?"

"So far, we have not harmed you."

We spent the late evening chatting. Both of us were in shorts, and I kept my legs far from him. He didn't mind the distance I kept myself away from him, and I was somewhat annoyed that he didn't come closer to me. I remember Bianca, my *de facto* counselor, told me for the first three nights, don't matter how lonely I feel, I should sleep upstairs and do not go downstairs at nights because I will be tempted to lie with Bill. She told me I should play hard to get. But that was real torture because my body wanted him from the day I saw him in Brooklyn.

I prayed for the third night, and that night was, to me, like a year away. Then he spoke in the living room.

"Élla Willa, did you go to see your friend, Dr. Joanna Napoli, in New Orleans?"

His question changed my sexual mood. "I did! I did! I spent a week with her in her palace on Lowerline Street, a very plush neighborhood, lined with trees, and beautified with flowers of every hue." I was excited to boast about my friend's prosperity. "My bedroom for that week was as big as a stadium." It was big, but my hyperbole was excessive.

"Then Dr. Napoli really lives the good life. Where did you know her?"

"We are the offspring of Caribbean parents. Her parents are from Jamaica, the land of wood and water, and my parents are from Trinidad and Tobago, the land of the humming bird. We were in grade school together; we were teenagers together; high schoolers together. She was smarter than I. She got into Princeton; I did not. I got into NYU. And when she graduated with a Ph.D. in molecular biology, I insisted, though she protested, on calling her Dr. Jo."

"What did you and Dr. Jo talk about?"

"Mostly about men's lies and their libidos."

"That sounds interesting." He looked at me.

"I told Dr. Jo about you."

"What you told her about me?"

"I told her I liked you from the minute I saw you."

"What is so special about me?"

"Your whiteness. I ended the conversation about your whiteness with her because I was driving and looking for an easy spot to park near to Palace Café. I like Palace Café flavor of New Orleans cookbook."

"Ella Willa, I ate and drank there three years ago when I visited New Orleans for the first time. I went to New Orleans on business. What did you and Dr. Jo order before eating?"

"From their Specialty Creations, I ordered a palace planters punch which is old New Orleans amber rum, cardamom, orgeat, vanilla brandy and lemon. Dr. Jo ordered the Painkiller which is plantation pineapple stiggins' fancy dark rum, Pusser's rum, cream of coconut, orange, and pineapple cocktail, served in a Tiki mug.

"Bill, with the third drink, we started to prattle. I asked Dr. Jo where she met her husband."

"She said, 'I met Victorio Napoli in a bar. I learned to hold my liquor at Princeton, and I could see Vic was surprised at the way I drank without getting drunk. Sometimes I was so f--kin stressed because nothing I did in the lab was working out. To feel better I went to the nearby bar to relax my brain. And there I met Vic. He was very quiet, and I like a quiet man. My parents told me when

I was a child their happiest hour was when I fell asleep because from the time I came home from school in grade one I never stopped talking. I talked about everything that took place in school, in the playground, on the bus home, and everywhere. I talked about everything until I fell asleep. And there was this man who listened at me as my poor parents did when I was a child; and now I was talking about my frustrated day in the lab. I looked at his rosy cheeks and felt to pinch them.'"

I smiled and said, "Dr. Jo, who spoke first?"

"I can't remember, Ella Willa."

"Is he a brother, Dr. Jo?" I rubbed the index finger of my right hand on the back-hand side of my left palm.

She answered quickly. "No, Ella Willa. Color is not my problem. He is a human being as far as I could re-member. When I tell the brothers I go to Princeton, they drop me as a hot brick. I guess they suffer from knowl-edge complex."

"Are you telling me the brothers are not human be-ings, Dr. Jo?"

"Ella Willa, you know what I mean. The brothers stay away from strong, black sisters."

"Dr. Jo, you have been coming by me since you were a little girl, and you know Pappy will flip on his head to know I'm dating a white boy, or a white gentleman."

"Not my parents! The color of a person's skin was never their problem. You and I are black; your complex-ion is a little lighter than mine. We are in our mid-thir-ties. For the years you didn't see me, I always dated out of my race. I always dated vanilla and whiteness. Probably I have a magnet that draws them. So don't let your next question be: 'Dr. Jo, whom do you prefer in bed—whiteness/vanilla or blackness?' I have nothing to compare, Ella Willa. Today I will pick up the check."

"One more question. Where did you get married, Dr. Jo?"

"In Las Vegas."

"I hope I have your luck, girl, to meet an angel as Vic. I have this love for a man burning inside of me that I want to give to one who will truly love me, and I hope William Baxter will be that man." We knocked glasses.

I stopped telling Bill about the conversation between Dr. Jo and me, and I addressed him. "Bill, do you want me to answer the question about your whiteness?" He smiled. "Not today. But one day I will ask you why your Pappy hates white people."

The night, that I had prayed to come, had come, and Bianca's advice was at the fore of my memory.

Bill and I had a sumptuous dinner. I had two glasses of wine. I could feel the sexual effect of the wine in every part of my body. But I was listening to my sister's voice in my ear: Ella Willa, wear the lingerie I bought you. Wait till the clock strikes midnight, then go downstairs and force yourself on his twin bed. You can use your old trick of letting your nipples do the talking, and I am now using that trick too. If your hard nipples are on his back, let them stay there for a while and then turn him around and let the show begin. Don't let geography and culture have a battle. Bring them together.

I went upstairs and showered quickly. I creamed my body thoroughly and perfumed it in the right places, and just the thought of what I soon will be doing caused a slight liquid to secrete from me. All I wore was a negligee without bra and an undersized panty that accentuated my arse. Walking downstairs the lighting on the stairway was dim, and I held the rail to prevent me from slipping in my high, backless, heels. I had watched pornos, and the women in pornos always wear heels during their sexual acts. I walked on my insteps, and as I got closer to the twin bed, I saw Bill's toes; his naked body was visible. He slept on his back at the right edge of the bed, and even dumb I knew that he knew I would be coming to join him on the space he left unoccupied. He, too, was waiting on that day to come.

The nipples of my breast did the talking as I pulled him with my left hand flush on me, and his mouth opened for air. My tongue filled his mouth and he bit my tongue softly. I wanted to talk but he won't let me. I felt the hardness of his organ rising but he wouldn't put it in. I wanted to climb on him and put it in but he preferred to torture me.

His was an art that I'd never experienced. The black men I knew boasted on the incessant jabs from their penis, but Bill's tongue jabbed harder, and longer. I moved like a feather in the wind, aimlessly. He wet my body with saliva, and when I thought he was over his gristle found its way into my wet space, warm and moist. He went to work. I screamed for joy. His breath was short and quiet. Mine was loud. Geography and culture meshed. Poetry had no lines but ours. His brush did contours on my body like railroads on a map tracing all the hills, valleys, and hideouts. He found the hideouts, and I was happy when he found them. I wanted to say, "I love you," but I didn't. I wanted him to say those three words first. If he didn't say them, I'd ask him why.

Then I remember a prostitute friend told me I should never force a man to do anything or say something, except on his own volition. The man who says I love you first, most times says it glibly; the man who delays saying it could be waiting for the woman to say it. I realized during that feeling of ecstasy that living in the present could be what will happen in the future if I play the game right, as Bianca had advised. Bill took me in his arms and I forgot what I was thinking when he played with my nipples, hard as bricks. His arms were muscular; his hands were rough; and my nipples loved his rough fingers.

"Ella Willa, if I say I love you, would you believe me?"

I did not answer. I ran my fingers on his hairy chest, and I let my fingers continue south. I touched his penis, and it was hard. "Bill, did you use Viagra because you knew I was coming tonight to sleep with you?"

"I read that stuff may damage my eyesight, and I want to see you for the rest of my life."

"What part of me you want to see most?"

He did his talking with his fingers. He cuffed my breasts with both hands, pulled the hairs on my pearl, gently, and asked, "Do you like what I'm doing to Eve's body?"

I smiled. "Yes, Adam."

"If you don't like that, I'll do something else."

"Like what?"

"You want to see how strong I am?"

"By doing what?"

Before my question ended, he lifted my naked, one-hundred-forty-pound body, ran upstairs, dropped me gently on the king-sized bed, and found my damp pearl. His penis was a non-stop piston revving my engine. I took the palm of his right hand and brought it to my mouth. I groaned with joy, and I spoke with fits-and-starts. I didn't wait for him to say the three words, I love you. I said them. And we ended our performance.

"Ella Willa, I said them first. You are late, very late. I had two gifts for you, but since you are late in loving me, I'll only give you the second gift when Bianca gives you your passport to leave London."

"The custodian of my passport forgot Pappy expect-ed me home a year ago."

"To continue his curfew on what time you should be home?"

"And to make his breakfast, lunch, and dinner."

"Bianca told me Pappy was waiting on a golden woman. Did she come?"

"Yes."

"Well, he doesn't need you to come back to spoil his romance."

"Let's sleep." I slipped into his arms, and we fell asleep.

The sun came shining on us next morning.

He spoke. "I want you to accompany me to my doctor tomorrow."

"Going to get circumcised?"

He laughed. "What was your observation of me last night, Ella Willa?"

"We waited too long to tell each other I love you. Why do you want me to accompany you to the doctor?"

"I don't think I'm good sexually as before."

"Before you were better than what you did last night? You and I are Generation X children. Wait until you are a boomer to complain."

"Boomers and Generation X's die from MS."

My heart asked my brain: Why is he talking about multiple sclerosis? "Bill, what are the signs?"

"Fatigue. Of late, I'm easily worn out after physical activity. As a car salesman and manager of my business, I can't hustle as before. My sales are dropping."

"What else is your self-analysis?"

"Sensory changes."

"To be exact?"

"Numbness, mood changes."

"I noticed that, but I thought I did something that you did not like, and I was wondering what it was that I did."

"Soon you will be noticing my sexual issues in months to come."

"Men use Viagra and other stuffs. Why can't you use them when that time comes?"

"Using that stuff would not help my case."

"In your last visit, have you discussed these signs with your doctor?"

"No."

"Your medical history should be private. Why do you want to take me to the doctor with you to hear your medical deficiencies?"

"To give me courage. I know what my doctor is going to say."

"Bill, Bill, Bill, be an optimist. Whatever the outcome, if you want me to stay and take care of you, I will."

"Can we change the subject?"

I kissed him. "Can we come out of our birthday suits?" We jumped out of bed and danced as if disco music was playing.

"I'm taking you to the Tower of London today to see the Queen's jewels."

"I do not want to go there."

"Why?"

"Bianca took me there three years ago, and I was pissing mad when I looked into those guarded glass cages and saw the jewels England plundered from her colonies."

"Well, I'll take you on a Thames River sightseeing

cruise."

"Do I have to dress up for that cruise?"

"Did you bring the outfit I met you in at Atlantic Avenue?"

"Yes."

"Wear that. But you won't be able to run home to beat Pappy's curfew."

I looked into his eyes, and he looked away trying not to show his emotions but I could see the doctor's visit was on his mind. We had breakfast. I walked around the living room, and I saw a pack of cards.

"Billy boy, my only lover, the only card game I know is Go-To-Pack. Come sit on my lap and play."

"I'm one sixty. I'm too heavy for you."

"I held you last night on my belly."

"I forgot."

We played six games. The score was even.

"Ella Willa, where are we sleeping tonight?"

"Downstairs on the twin bed where you can't hide from me."

"Let's have some music." He put in a disk. "I like this tune. You know who that is?"

"Eric Reed playing *Flamenco Sketches*. Whenever I hear jazz, I miss Pappy."

"Call your sister and both of you can cry over your Pappy. I'm stepping out."

"Would you be long?"

"Not at all."

7

It was springtime, and my third visit to London. My visits were always in April. April 1 was cold and windy, but I liked the wind in my face. Bill and I held hands. We visited Kew Garden and the blaze of colors had me stunned of what nature can do for our happiness. The rock garden is one of the places I've been dreaming to see once more since I first saw it three years ago. We walked by the water falls and streams. We stood still admiring a carpet of alpine flowers in pink, purple, and white. Bill kissed me for each color. The flowering cherry trees had me following and counting them. Bill let go my hands, and I walked fifty yards or more admiring the beauty of the landscape. I danced on the cherry walk leading to the Temperate House. I waited for Bill at the entrance of the Temperate House.

"Look up, Bill, something is going to fall on you!"

He looked up.

"April 1, All Fools' Day. You are a fool."

"I'll always be your fool, Ella Willa."

"Bill, I'll be your bigger fool."

We hugged, kissed, and then we sat on a bench. We laughed. We giggled. We tickled each other, and we kissed countless times. We made it fun by describing passersby. He described the women, and I described the men. I showed him a man I'd like to flirt with. He showed me a beautiful women and said he'd never flirt with her.

"Why, Bill?"

"Her boobs are too small, and I suspect she will not make loud noise when we are doing it."

"How do you know that?"

"Because I know a bubbleologist when I see one."

"Who is that?"

"A woman who loves to make bubbles in a tub and not in the bedroom."

"You had one?"

"Couple."

"Am I one of the couple?"

"You don't make bubbles. You burst bubbles."

He kissed me deep. I paid him back.

"Bill, in what way do you show your prejudice?" He was a bit shocked by my question. He looked at me intently when he answered my question

"When I'm trying too hard not to show it."

"Give me an example."

"When I first saw you in Brooklyn, I was standing by the old Williamsburgh Bank Building. To get to talk to you, I crossed the street, forced my way through two parked cars and was almost through. A black woman was about to get in the same space with me, and I reversed my body back to the beginning of the space to let her in. She said, 'You don't have to do that!' That's all right, Miss, I said.'"

"She replied, 'White Boy, are you trying to show this black woman that you are not prejudice by rendering the space for me? And you won't tell me to go to the back of the bus as you crackers once told black people.'"

"I was stumped by what she said."

"Bill, she is a f--kin fool. Some of us bring up race without a reason to. I hate people like that whether they are black or white, or whatever color they."

"April 1, All Fools' Day. I made up that story. You are now the fool. Two fools in the park." He ran.

"So you got me. That's really unfair. You are a liar just as my President." I ran after him. When I reached close to him, he ran farther. Then he stopped, and I held him tightly. "So you are practicing to run away from me and be a congenital liar as my President."

"From what I've read in the London press, I could never match your President's lies. And I will never run away from you."

"But you just did."

"I did?"

"Yes, you did."

"That's the last time I'll be doing that."

"Promise?"

"I promise. I have a great idea."

"What?"

"Let us go by Bianca when we leave here. I have a secret to share with her."

"You two are ganging up on me."

"Not really. I will be making a call to an associate in Brooklyn, and she knows about that call."

"Is that so?"

"That is so."

"I hope when we go by her, she will give me my passport. My visa for England will expire in two months."

"So?"

"I don't want my visa to expire."

"I'll put in a word for you."

"To Bianca or to Immigration?"

"To Bianca."

We had a wonderful time in Kew Garden, and I slept all the way to Bianca's apartment. I could smell her stewed meat as Bill turned into Alexandra Road, and I told Bill I know what Bianca is cooking, and to bet me five pounds.

"If you lose, you will have to sleep upstairs by yourself for a week."

"Let's call off that bet."

I pounded his arms until he got to the front door. "You are not a nice man. I hate you."

Bianca opened the door and kissed Bill first.

"Bianca, why did you kiss this man before you kissed your little sister? He tricked me in Kew Garden. Don't call him Bill. Call him White Boy."

"Ella Willa, I don't have all Pappy's habits. I will not call him so."

"Bianca, a woman called him White Boy in Brooklyn, and he didn't object being called so."

"Bill, why did that woman call you White Boy in Brooklyn?" Bianca asked.

"Wait till April 1 next year, and I will tell you why."

"I will be in Brooklyn by that time," I said.

"You are going to travel without your passport?" Bianca asked.

"I am an American. I can leave to go home without a passport. At JFK I'll tell the Customs Officer someone stole my passport, and I will be let in."

"With Donald Trump's new rules, Customs will not admit you. You are an illegal Mexican," Bill said, and he laughed endlessly. He poked fun at Trump's America's Immigration laws.

"I will tell Pappy to come and rescue me." While they laughed riotously, I went into the many pots, served myself, and told Bill I will not serve him because he and Bianca hid my passport.

The dinner was delicious. We trash talked. Bill said he will wash the dishes. Bianca said she does want the white boy in her kitchen, and laughed. Then she asked me if I found this white boy in the laundromat. I told her that I'm like Gail King, Oprah's friend. She said she will never pick up a man in a laundromat. The mere fact that he is coming there to wash his clothes means he doesn't have a washing machine, and that means he has little means. Those are not Gail King's exact words, but that is what she meant. Sister, because of you, I'm learning how to choose a man with means."

Our laughter echoed through the houses on Alexandra Road. To end our laughter, Bianca told me she is going to call Pappy.

"Why are you going to call Pappy?" I asked.

"To find out if he has company."

"He is a big man. I hope you don't want to panhandle to pay for your Ph.D. studies. Let your man or men help you. You can sell sex for money. At thirty two, you should be out of the entitlement generation."

Bianca called Pappy, put the phone on speaker, and handed me the phone. "Pappy, this is Ella Willa. How are you? I miss you."

He had no excitement in his voice. "I am quite well. When are you coming home?"

"I lost my passport, and I am making arrangements to get one from the American Embassy." We spoke for a long time. "Pappy, Bianca wants to speak with you." I handed Bianca the phone.

Without salutation, Bianca went directly to the question on her mind. "Pappy, is that woman there with you?"

"Yes."

"Do you like her?"

"Yes."

"Does she go home at nights?"

"No; she sleeps over to keep my company."

"I want to speak to her."

"Judith, someone wants to speak to you." Pappy hands Judith the phone.

"Hello. Who is this?"

"I am Bianca Wilcox."

"You are the one your Father never tamed."

"Yes; I am the animal." Bianca raised her voice.

"Bianca, I am sorry. What I meant is although you are five years younger than Ella Willa you are the leader."

"Pappy, informed you well. Let me speak to Pappy, if you don't mind."

"Mr. Wilcox, the other daughter wants to speak to you." She handed him the phone.

"Hello."

"Pappy, that bitch calls me the other daughter. Doesn't she know my name?"

"Bianca, be calm. Lower your voice," Pappy begged.

"I want to speak to that bitch before I speak to you."

"Another time, Bianca. But I will let her know that you have a name, and she should address you by your name. I am so proud of you. Let me know when you are getting your Ph.D. I will be there for your graduation. Did you get the money I sent for you?"

"Yes, Pappy. But don't bring that bitch when you are coming to my graduation."

"Okay. How are you and Ella Willa getting on?"

"Great. Pappy, someone wants to speak to you." She hands Bill the phone.

"Good evening, Mr. Wilcox. My name is William

Baxter. I am deeply in love with your daughter."

"Which one?"

"Your first born."

"She has a name."

"Sorry, sir. Ella Willa Wilcox. I am asking you for her hand in marriage."

"Over the phone? I don't know who you are. I don't know if you are a cockney lay-about, a bandit, or a con man. Come to my house where I can see you. Are you white or black?"

"White."

Pappy hung up. I took the phone from Bill, and I would not let Bianca call Pappy because I knew Bianca would tell Pappy things that I did not want Bill to hear. I cried aloud. Bill hugged me. I pulled away from him and blasted Bianca with obscenity. "Bianca, I'm f--kin mad. How could you do this to Bill? You know how Pappy hates white people since he could have been sent to prison because of the lie of that white-bitch teller in the bank."

Bill hugged me gently and kissed me softly. "What that woman did—I mean that white-bitch teller?"

My speech was broken. "A thief had broken into our house and stole Pappy's bank book. That bold thief went to the bank, outsmarted the teller who, probably, did not check for proper ID from the thief. The thief withdrew the total sum of money in Pappy's bank book. Bianca was ill, and Pappy wanted money to take her to a doctor. He always took us to private doctors. Pappy looked in the pockets of his old, black jacket in the closet where he always kept his bank book. My Mother was still alive, and he asked her if she hid his bank book. She said no.

"Pappy rushed to the bank and told the bank manager he cannot find his bank book. He gave the bank manager his ID. The manager asked him where he works. He told the bank manager the name of the law firm where he works, and Pappy also told the bank manager the account number of his bank book, and the balance in his bank book.

"The bank manager left and brought back a white woman. The manager said to the white woman, he called her name, 'Is this the man who drew all the money from his bank account last week?' She said, 'Yes.' The manager looked her in the eye and raised his voice. 'Are you sure this is the man you paid all the money to last week?' The white teller said, 'I am one hundred percent sure this is the black man I paid.' Pappy said to the bank manager what the teller is saying could not be true because he was not in the bank for over a month to withdraw any money from his bank book. Pappy could not convince the bank manager that the teller was lying on him. Pappy left the bank, went to the public phone booth, spoke to our Mother and told her his calamity. After Pappy and our Mother spoke, he went and prayed in Trinity Cathedral at the corner of Broadway and Wall Street, and asked God to let the bank manager believe him. Then he went to work.

"As Pappy pulled out his chair on his job and sat down, the office manager of the law firm asked him for the office key. (All the employees of that law firm are given an office key.) Pappy gave his office key to the office manager. The office manager told Pappy to pick up his bag. Pappy picked up his bag. The office manager said, 'Let's go.' Pappy said, "Go where, sir?' The office manager said, 'Follow me.' He walked Pappy to the elevator, pressed the down button, and said, 'James, the company is downsizing. We have to let you go.' He handed Pappy an envelope with a letter within which states James Wilcox can use the law firm as reference for unemployment compensation.

"My belief is: When Pappy left the bank, the bank manager called Pappy's job manager at the Wall Street law firm and told the manager what James Wilcox did. That Wall Street law firm would not risk having a bank robber as James Wilcox in their employ. Thus, the law firm's safest way to get rid of Mr. Wilcox without being served a lawsuit was to tell Mr. Wilcox the company is downsizing."

I cried aloud as I related that sad day in Pappy's life to Bill. Bill put me to sit on his lap, and I continued speaking.

"Bill, Pappy worked some months, I can't remember how many months, for a lawyer free of charge as payment for the lawyer's fees. Months later all the money was put back in Pappy's bank account. The lawyer told Pappy robbing the bank is a federal crime, and he would have had to spend a long time in prison if what the bank's teller had said about him was true.

"The fact that Pappy could have been sent to prison by the blatant lie of one white woman is why Pappy hates white people. I told Pappy one swallow doesn't make a summer, and one lying white teller doesn't make every white teller a pathological liar. Bill, I will never tell you Pappy's answer to me for my so-called logical thinking."

"Ella Willa, you don't have to tell me. The way your Pappy slammed down the phone on me, a white man, because I want to marry his beautiful daughter, I could imagine the expletives he used in describing that white teller who wanted him to go to prison. Ella Willa, I have a subjective reason for the teller's lie."

Shocked, I looked at him. "What! What?"

"My dear Ella Willa Wilcox, that bank teller is not a pathological liar. She knew she lied. But she also knew if she told the truth, and the truth is she gave the wrong black man Pappy's money because she did not check the wrong black man's identification properly, that would cost her to lose her job. Probably she is a single mother, deep in debt; probably she is taking care of two old, sick parents and needs money to upkeep them, and if she loses her job that would be a bad thing for her family. She would have no money to upkeep her family. Probably her education is limited, and she would not be able to get a job quickly. All these things are possible."

"My dear William Baxter of London, England, she thought of her own skin, not the skin of my Father's going to prison, and dying in prison." I looked at Bill, shook my head, showed my anger, and said, "Is your subjective finding a footnote to life?" He didn't answer, and I continued. "Pappy got another job at another prestigious Wall Street law firm, and he loved his white-woman boss. He worked in that Wall Street law firm for eighteen years, and retired from that law firm with a good pension. Up to this day he and his white-woman boss keep in touch; and in the past she had invited Pappy home for dinner."

"Had he returned her kindness and invited her to his home for dinner?" Bill looked at me.

"No." I knew why Bill asked that question.

I felt much better as I poured out my soul to Bill, and I said to Bianca, "Bill asked me to go with him to see his doctor."

"Ella Willa, why is he taking you to see a gynecologist?"

There was laughter for the first time since Pappy slammed the phone down on Bill.

"Little sister, Bill and I don't have sex so there is no reason for him to take me to a gynecologist."

"Big sister, didn't I tell you when I sent you to have companionate marriage with him that after three days you should not sleep upstairs by yourself on that giant bed? You should sleep downstairs on the little twin bed where your bodies will rub uncontrollably on each other and both bodies will generate heat and that heat from both bodies will make both of you have sex, and more sex."

"Bianca, because of you ..." I laughed aloud, and could not stop laughing. Bill's laughter must have reached the fire engine two blocks away.

There was laughter and more laughter, and I was very happy how the evening was progressing. I got off Bill's lap and said, "Bianca, Bill thinks he has all the symptoms for MS. He says in five to ten years he may be in a wheelchair." I looked at Bill and changed the subject. "Bill, why did you let Bianca make you call Pappy?"

"Because I know you'd never let me call him."

"Did you like the reception you got from him?"

"The next time I ask that question, I will be in front of him. I think he was right to hang up on me but he showed his innate prejudice by not inviting his white-woman boss home to his house for dinner."

Bianca spoke. "Bill, I'm the daughter Pappy never tamed. Pappy will respect you the next time you speak to him. And he will have to apologize to you for his nasty behavior today. And, as for that bitch, who is sleeping with Pappy on my Mother's bed, who called me 'the Other Untamed Daughter,' we'll meet again before high noon."

8

❝Ella Willa, on Monday I'm taking you on the job to learn my business that will soon be our business. You will be handling the export-import side of the business and person-to-person discussions with your astuteness, which I think is your forté. You must be able to tell customers everything that Cooper offers—Mini 3-door hatch, 5-door hatch, countryman, clubman, and convertible; that Cooper is available in seven fuel-efficient models, and you have to know them and speak about them with alacrity. You have to study all aspects of the business." He looked at me with his business face which I've seen for the first time so to counter that look I put on my acting face.

"Honey, would I be paid by you?"

"No. You are a visitor without a visa. I don't want to break the law. But you will be given the combination to my safe. And you could pay yourself."

"Could I pay myself a bonus for the unsafe sex on

the twin bed?"

"Deduct for the days you are in red."

"Cockney lay-about, you are very nasty." I rushed him, and he hugged me.

"Today is Thursday. Let's invite Bianca over tomorrow."

"I don't think I'll like that. She made you look bad in front of Pappy."

"Pappy was in Brooklyn when he slammed the phone on me. I was not in front of him."

"How do you like him calling you a cockney lay-about?"

"The ebbs and flows of the slime from humans' tongues were there since the time of Adam, Eve, and the Serpent."

"I don't want to hear anything biblical tonight, only if you will know my body is as sinful as men in biblical times. My movements on your thorax would be a hot girl's language."

He looked at me.

"You have been avoiding sleeping on the twin bed with me. Why? Why?"

He did not answer.

"What did your doctor tell you?"

"I don't want to talk about it now."

"I walk with my New York driving license, and I know how to drive on the left-hand side of the street. Let me take you for a ride in the countryman."

"Where?"

"Put on clothes." I was already dressed. He liked my suggestion. He put on clothes quickly; we walked to the mini countryman; and he sat on the passenger's seat. "Bill, I'm going to drive you on a road that's built for speed."

I sat at the wheel for two minutes. "If you kiss me, I'll change my mind and let you drive me on the A13 Highway that will take us back to Alexandra Road."

"How do you know of that route?"

"I'm from Brooklyn. Brooklynites know how to get in and out of a situation if they're in a jam."

"You are a broad not to be trusted."

"I'm so glad you know one of my better traits."

He gave me two deep kisses. "Bill, it's October. Take me to the best place to see the Northern Lights."

"I'll take you there for our honeymoon." His cell rang. "Hello."

"Hi, Bill. I quit studies for the weekend. I'm taking you and Ella Willa to East End Social to meet great company, eat great food, drink wine, and dance vulgarly. It is east and they say east is the best. I don't have to pretend that I am Eastic. I live on Alexandra Street, and I am a member of the club. And since you will be with me, you don't have to shout when you get there and say you like jellied eels."

"Bianca, that's a deal. Ella Willa was taking me for a ride, but I'll give it a rain check."

"Pick me up by nine."

"No Brexit or Trump politics tonight."

"I can't promise you that."

At ten thirty I rang her bell. We knew she's always an hour and a half late. She walked to the Cooper. "Bill, where's your hipster beard? Without it, you wouldn't belong."

"Bianca, that's all right. He belongs to me, not to you Eastic folks."

"The cockney lay-about doesn't?" Bill asked.

Our laughter was plentiful all the way to the club, and in the club people excelled in styles and fashions. But after laughter, riotous music, and vulgar dancing, there was a familial storm: An old flame of Bill's, a Mediterranean woman in red (I later learned her name) was there. Bill said their romance was over, but the old flame in red behaved as if she is hotly burning for him. She brought a glass of wine, sipped from the glass, and handed the glass to Bill. I knocked the glass from his hand, dirty her beautiful dress, and said, "Who the f--k is this bitch?" He did not answer. Bianca was dancing, her hips sinfully inviting. But wherever she was in a crowd her eyes were on me. She never lost that habit from childhood.

I am not a fighter with my fists, but my tongue with words is sharper than a new razor. Somehow I controlled myself. I knew this was not a night to start a fight because I knew if I start a fight Bianca would end it with blood. I held Bill's hand and moved him away and sat in a chair with my back turned where Bianca could not read my countenance. She is good at that. She knew when Pappy provoked me without my telling her. She knew when I was bullied by Westy without my telling her, and I could not tell her when I was feeling ill because she became my nurse around the clock and watched me like a guard dog.

The woman in red followed us with another drink in her hand. I was not scared because I knew the culture of the club by looking at the patrons. They looked congenial, and I suspected that this woman in red was not a riotous Eastic. I thought probably this woman in red wants to be nice to me seeing that she lost her man, and she wants to let me know she is a fair loser. But why, I thought, is she following us with another glass of wine in her hand?

Bill will not let go my hand. Reggae music was blasting, and I wanted to dance. I looked at him, and he glided his eyes to the woman in red. My eyes followed him, and I glanced at her too. She is a beautiful woman with Mediterranean complexion. She could win any beauty contest, and I became extremely jealous of her beauty. Immediately, I hated that I came to the club to see the kind of woman Bill was once in love with. Probably he still sees her when he leaves me home. Probably he gives her money. Probably he gave her a car, the one of her choice, regardless of the cost. Probably they have a child, unknown to me. All those thoughts crossed my mind, and I pulled my hand away from him. Now my eyes were fully transfixed on that Mediterranean woman. Another woman just as beautiful sat next to her, and they chatted. My angry attitude told me they were talking about me saying, "That black American bitch with natural hair, probably she cannot afford to buy synthetic hair as other black women; probably she's Bill's helper that he f--ks in exchange for lodging."

Why was I getting so ridiculously jealous and thinking so low of myself? Bill wanted to dance. But all I was thinking was this woman in red is so much more beautiful than I. At the end of that thought, Bianca ended dancing, came to my table, and said, "Ella Willa, I was looking for you. Why you moved from where you were sitting?"

"Where I am sitting now is better," I said.

"Better how?"

"Just better."

Bianca said, "Bill, why are you two sitting, not dancing, and not drinking?"

Bill replied, "Bianca, I was waiting on you to buy drinks. What would you have?"

"You know what I like."

Bill looked at me. "What would you have, Ella Willa?"

"Businessman Bill, buy a brimming glass of wine for the woman in red. Don't forget I purposely spilled her glass of wine on her and soiled her million-dollar dress; and buy a whiskey straight for me."

Bianca looked me in my eyes. "What the f--k you did to that woman?"

"I purposely spilled her glass of wine on her dress because she sipped on the glass and then gave Bill to drink."

"Whose drink you spilled?"

"I don't know her name. That Mediterranean look-ing woman." I pointed to the woman.

Bill brought our drinks. And I saw when he spoke to the woman in red, and handed her a glass of wine. As Bill handed me my glass, I threw the whiskey down my throat.

Bianca looked at Bill and me. She said, "Bill what took place while I was dancing?"

Bill did not lie. In fact, he could not lie because of the way Bianca looked in his eyes. He said, "Benadet-ta brought her wine for me to take a sip, and Ella Willa slapped the glass out of my hand and the wine dirty Be-nadetta's dress."

"Who's Benadetta?" Bianca asked.

He pointed. "The woman sitting over there in red."

Bianca looked at the woman in red. "She's a really pretty woman. She is your lover?"

"She's my friend, not my lover."

"When did the loving part ended, Bill?"

"Just before Ella Willa came. I'd told you I ended all my philanderings when you assured me Ella Willa was coming."

"Tell me her name again to check my memory?"

"Benadetta."

"Bill, do you want to go and apologize to Benadetta for my sister's jealous behavior? This club does not ca-ter for riff-raffs. I have been coming here for a very long time. If that woman makes a report, that report will be put on my membership card and..."

Before Bianca sentence ended, Bill said, "Bianca, she will never make a report."

"How do you know, Bill?"

"Believe me, she will never make a report on you for Ella Willa's stupid behavior."

"Why?"

"She wouldn't want her husband to know where she is tonight. He will never come here. To him, here's a dump." He smiled. "Let's dance, Ella Willa, my only love."

Bianca spoke. "Not now, Bill. Go and dance with Benadetta. Don't rush to come back. I hate a man who disses an old friend for a new friend. My sister and I will have a woman-to-woman talk in your absence."

When Bill left, Bianca changed the seating of the chairs. She let me sit on a chair with my back facing Bill and Benadetta when they danced. She did not want me to see the expression on Benadetta's face when she danced with Bill.

Bianca began scolding me. "Ella Willa, why did you throw your whiskey down your throat like a woman in pain who lost her lover?"

"I was thirsty."

"For your lost lover?"

I did not answer.

"You think you are losing Bill?"

"I never owned him. He's not chattel."

"Ella Willa, you will never win a love battle with blows. Even if a man loves you to death, his love will dry up because he'll see a problem lying in wait, and that problem will be you and your stupid jealousy. You didn't like Westy's stupidity but you hated his jealousy more." She looked at me, chuckled, and knocked my glass. I reciprocated and knocked her glass.

Bill came back from dancing, and I saw when he kissed Benadetta on her cheeks.

"Sisters, were you laughing at moi?"

"Who is Moi?" Bianca and I laughed aloud.

"Moi is I," Bill said and thought his answer would check our laughter.

Bianca held Bill's hand and said to me, "Little sister, I'm going to show this white boy Brooklyn's dirty dancing." She winked at me.

As I sat and drank my rum and coke, my childhood crossed my mind: Pappy's strictness and overtaxed discipline came to mind first. I suffered from sexual taboos, and it seems now older than then sexual taboos still have an effect on me as when I was with Westy. Westy wanted me to perform acts that I heard other women love, but those were the acts that Father frowned about. He did not tell me to my face but I heard his conversations with his friends on the phone. Probably he spoke loudly for me to hear. I remember I touched certain parts of my body as if I were a stranger to my body, and I whispered to myself when I had a sexual desire whether it was the stranger doing it. I suddenly realized that my love had two layers—love for me, and love for others. Sexual ethics and sexual institutions should no longer dictate my liking, and my feelings should be my feelings, nobody's.

My new thinking was telling me never will I be such an ass to think Bill is my chattel or Bill loves me only. My goal would be if Bill only wants to put me in bed for his pleasure, his bed will not be my only bed. My approach to sex will not be linked to taboos for I'm neither religious nor tribal. My sexual relations with Bill will have a large psychical thread; it will not be strictly physical. I will be evaluating my love in proportion to its depth from Bill's, or any lover for that matter.

Bianca and Bill were finished dancing as two drunken sailors but only Bianca came back to our table with two rum and coke. We knocked glasses, and she spoke. "Ella Willa, I want you to listen to every word I'm telling you. In London economic and sexual interests are intertwined and these Mediterranean women with yellow skins know how to work their charm. So if you think you will be going around and slapping all the women who hand Bill their glasses to taste their wine, you will always be a sore loser. When you lose your temper, you lose your smarts; it shows you are suffering from an inferiority complex, and your worth is less than those women with yellow skins.

"I am going to let the bandleader, my friend, Juju Blades, let you do a solo to show your talents as a singer and a keyboardist. Whenever you wanted favors from Pappy you used to sing a medley of songs and play the piano. I remember your favorite key was B flat. With the anger in your heart, I don't know what key you will sing in now. But go and break a leg, musically." She called Bill. "Bill, hold Ella Willa's hand and take her to the bandleader." She had planned that already. I suspected something was going on between her and Juju because from the time I had misbehaved, she had gone to speak with Juju, and Juju was looking at me as if I had committed a crime.

Bill handed me to Juju and said, "She's yours, Juju." I saw Bianca's eyes on me, and it was as if we were in the living room in our house in Brooklyn with Pappy in his easy chair cheering me. She started to make monkey face at me because she knew I excelled when she did that to get Pappy's half dollar which I would share with her; and now it was time for me to get Bill's favor and to love me only instead of that Mediterranean woman.

Juju handed me the microphone; I sat at the piano, ran the B flat scale, and rambled on the keys, not knowing what to play. *Fools Rush In Where Angels Fear to Tread* came on my E flat chord, and I began. I saw the joy in Bianca's face, and I opened with my lungs singing. I felt I was Ella Fitzgerald with a three-range octave. I heard the musicianship of Juju brushing his drums; Buddie, the bassist, pulled a deep string, and Jacko strumming his rhythm guitar. I purposely went off key and played a contrapuntal melody. I hit the notes *fools rush in* with a staccato touch, and *where angels fear to tread* with a legato feeling. Juju went Latin on the drums. I went crazy on the keys with chord changes and runs. I caught myself "swinging high energy style of jazz piano" as if I were John Colianni at Club Bonafide in New York, my favorite hangout. The crowd went wild when I ended. I stood and bowed to my audience. Bill ran to me, lifted me in the air as burnt offering, and kissed every spot on my face countless times. When I looked for the Mediterranean woman she was gone.

We drove home singing a medley of popular standards.

That night I tossed off my clothes, and he too could not wait. We fell into a billowing embrace. We left the lights on to give us heat, to see what we were doing to heighten our sexuality. We always leave the lights on when we want to be vulgar. The twin bed became smaller, and it made us one. Bill's long fingers grazed below me and the world was mine without fighting for it. I saw rainbows in the sky, and said, "I love you, Bill."

"I love you only, Ella Willa."

9

"Ella Willa, you always accompanied me to work to learn the quirks of the business; but today I am not going to work so you have to run the dealership and make all the decisions by yourself. Don't call me. I have called Gordon and Richard to open up for you. They are happy that you will be coming. They told me you are very nice, and they love to hear you boast about Brooklyn, and you said it is the capital of New York with your thunderous laughter. Gordon and Richard told me they laughed their asses out about the story you told them about the woman on the subway who gave her soaking, wet umbrella to a beggar to sell on the street instead of begging on the subway. Gordon told me he imitated your Brooklynite-mudder-effs cursing that the beggar gave that upstart woman."

"Bill, Gordon had the Brooklyn accent down right. That uppity bitch was out of place with her attitude. The beggar was right to cuss her. Gordon told me he was glad he broke up with the woman from Seychelles and married Celia. I don't know why Richard made it his duty to tell me his wife is white. The half day you left me with them, we closed the business for an hour and ate on the same table. Somehow they trusted me with their personal lives. At times, I was shocked what Richard told me about their daughter, Leah, black as he, and their son, Mack, white as his wife. On the street, his wife holds Mack's hand, and he holds Leah's hand. He told me he makes it his business to watch passersby looking at them. Gordon said he and his new wife, Celia, love to increase the nosy people's interest in them by doing odd things and making noisy comments."

"Like what, Ella Willa?"

"Celia will tell Gordon in a loud voice, 'Why are you so stupid, boy? You can't count.' He would answer, 'That's why I married you, fool. You are more stupid than dead grass.'"

"Ella Willa, I don't like their style."

"Neither do I, Bill."

Bill remained in his T-shirt and underpants and read the newspaper from back to front, and he crushes the sheets he reads. I went in the tub. As the froth and foams soaked my body I wondered why Bill was not going to work: Did his doctor give him bad news about his body? Does he want to see how I can handle his business in his absence? Did he tell Richard and Gordon to have an eye on me? Does he have a date with that Mediterranean woman?

I forgot I was in the tub. My mind roamed to my Father and his woman, and if they love each other because my Father was still mourning for my Mother whom he loved dearly. Then the corollary: If Bill and Pappy fall sick at the same time whom should I rush to: One is my flesh and blood and fatherhood is not unknown, and the dominion of my Father is sacred; the other is the man I love deeper than the ocean, and I know without a doubt he loves me and would give his last drop of blood to save my life. Would my faith in religion determine my choice? Why should it? Pappy was never religious, but my Mother was. She is dead; Pappy is alive. He says religion is superstition; she taught Bianca and me our faith is our religion. He would interrupt my Mother and say, "The sexual element in religion took the form of phallic worship." Mother hated when Pappy used big words and become blasphemous. I was dreaming when someone touched me.

"Ella Willa, get up. It's time to leave for work and beat the traffic. You have to drive slowly because you are not accustomed to driving on the left-hand side of the street. Wash the soap off your body. I prepared lunch for you, enough to share with Richard and Gordon."

"You are such a good man."

I was up, dressed as an executive, and I told Bill of a day at high school. "When I was at Erasmus Hall High School I always admired Miss Balford. A student had asked her, 'Miss Balford, what's your style of dressing?' Miss Balford answered, 'Executive, with my natural hair.'

The student said, 'What executive means?' Miss Balford replied, 'It's a corporate word to keep black women in line to straighten their hair. But mine will be natural always.'"

"Ella Willa, that's why you always go natural like Miss Balford?"

I looked him in his eyes. "What do you mean by always go natural like Miss Balford?"

He did not answer.

"How did your other black women carry their hair?"

"Carry their hair?"

"Yes, carry their hair."

"On their head, of course."

"It looked like mine?"

"No."

"Then describe it."

"It was processed, or the synthetic hair."

"Straight like yours?"

"Some."

"So you had many black women. What about your others?"

"Less straight."

"What do you want me to do with mine?"

"Nothing."

"Then why did you ask me that question?"

"For conversation's sake."

"You want me to process my hair?"

He did not answer.

"Do you want me to buy synthetic hair or get human hair from Brazil?" I raised my voice and started to take off my beautiful top. He rushed to stop me. I pushed his hands off me. He tried to say something, but my voice drowned his. "Give me the f--kin money to go to Bombay, India. Hair is cheaper there."

"Ella Willa, calm down. Your hair looks naturally beautiful. I like your executive style. Miss Balford was right. I read of black women in America who had to go to court to wear their hair natural."

"You bring up my natural hair because I am going to sell cars to corporate people with straight hair?"

"No such thing, Ella Willa. People with your hair have money too. Plenty f--kin money! Some of them have money to burn. Sometimes I'm afraid to bring up certain topics with you because you are extra sensitive." He came and buttoned my top. And he spoke softly. "American woman, you are more beautiful when you are annoyed. I hope a white guy gets you annoyed at the dealership today to see your beauty and buy two Mini Coopers." He kissed me on my forehead, sang *My Funny Valentine*, and when he got to the lines, 'Don't change your hair for me/ Not if you care for me, he rumpled my hair, ran and stood in front of the full-body mirror, took out the comb and brush from his pocket, handed them to me, and whispered in my ear, "Honey, am sorry for the way I explained myself. Do you love me still?" He knew his smile will melt me. And it did. If I were not late for work I would have changed my clothes and pull him on the twin bed.

He stretched his hand. "My name is Wyllie Longmoor."

I held his grip. "My name is Ella Willa Wilcox. I see that you were admiring the Mini Coopers. They are 4-cylinder, 2-wheel drive, manual transmission, red and black."

"Do you have puncture proof tires?"

"Yes and no. It depends on the type of driving you will be doing—country or city—and the size of the car. These tires come in sizes 17-22 inches, so if your car is too small the tire will not work. So in your case the Mini Cooper is too small for these tires."

"Is your vehicle maintenance free?"

"Yes, but you must come in every seven thousand miles for an oil change and tire rotation to keep the car running smoothly."

"I don't want it running smoothly; I want it efficiently."

I smiled.

"Do you have airbags and child safety seats?"

"Yes. The car comes standard with airbags; child safety seats would be considered an extra feature and would be a little more costly. How old is your child?"

"Seven years old."

"Your child is at the age where she can drive without safety seats."

"If I buy the car, do you provide rebate?"

"I'm glad you ask. For you, today, I will eliminate

all your import taxes and throw some money vouchers towards the price of the car."

"What about insurance? Insurance is very important. Can I have liability comprehensive and collision insurance?"

"Yes. Buying a new car requires full coverage."

"What kind of warranty do I receive with this vehicle?"

"You will have bumper to bumper coverage."

We spoke at length about prices, then we strayed into other subjects, and I saw he was very interested in buying a Cooper. I smiled and said, "Mr. Longmoor, now that we settled all your questions, how would you like to purchase your new car—cash or credit, Sir?"

"I walk with two checkbooks."

The sale was finalized after he took a test drive in the black Cooper.

He asked, "Where is William today?"

"I am he. I represent him."

"He is English. You are a black American woman selling English cars and pretending to be who you are not."

I did not know how to answer that question so I turn to politics, my favorite pastime. "I am an American but I'm not interfering in Brexit."

"Are you for or against Brexit?"

I did not answer because I did not know on whose side was he. And I wanted his sale.

"Can I see you again to discuss it?"

"If you are buying the red Coop for your woman, sure."

"I love smart, black, comely women. I want to buy it for you."

I knew his worth, but I pretended I did not understand his slant.

"I will be back to see you."

I was mum.

While driving home I was thinking of Bill's health more than anything else because I'd read up the signs of multiple sclerosis and had spoken to my friend, Frances, who is in a wheelchair and is suffering from MS.

10

"Bill, how come whenever I ask you to accompany you to the doctor you always send me to the dealership to sell cars?"

"Because you are a good salesman, and I hear you enjoy when the male customers flirt with you."

"I prefer you doing the flirting with me. I can't tell the last time you caressed me in bed."

"What about tonight?"

I pretended I did not hear him. "I have the Coop every day. You call Uber to take you to the doctor?"

"No."

"Who takes you?"

"A friend."

"That Mediterranean woman?"

"Yes."

"I thought you said that's over?"

"It is over. It's just friendship."

"Do you invite her upstairs when she comes to pick

you up?"

"No."

"Why?"

He looked at me, and I could see that he was thinking of how I slapped away her glass of wine from his hand in the club. I wondered if I should stop asking him questions about a woman who was his lover and believe that they are just friends. Bianca's advice was crawling not only in my brain but all over my body. Bill had prepared a sumptuous dinner but what was strange to me he didn't have a glass or two of wine. He likes wine, and he gave me the habit of having wine with dinner. Now I found a way to get him to divulge information. "Bill, your doctor told you to stop drinking because it is having a bad effect on one of the symptoms that is bad for your health?"

He did not answer.

"Why are you not responsive in bed?"

He did not answer.

"Why were you listening so attentively to what Montel Williams was saying in that American talk show?"

"The TV was on, but I was not really listening attentively."

"Do you know his disease?"

"Yes."

"What's it?"

"MS."

I got nervous, really nervous. Lord, I hope Bill is not in the advanced stage of MS. Then my mind went back to what I know of my friend, Frances, who has MS whom

I visited in Jamaica Hospital many times before coming to London. Frances had told me that in the early stage of multiple sclerosis she had lost interest in every-day activities that she once relished, and her tiredness was common. Then it came to mind Bill is like that now. He doesn't like to go to work, and his work was his life. He doesn't care to see me naked, and he has no interest to look at pornography with me.

I put my mind at ease by playing jazz. Bill had bought a keyboard after he saw my talent at the East Ham Club. At nights I begged him if I could play whatever he wanted to hear. He didn't care to hear me. I thought that his business at the other dealership that he thought I know very little about was not doing well. But that was not true. I kept the books and was in constant touch with the manager of that other dealership even though I had never seen him.

Bill was in deep thought in the living room, and I kissed him on his forehead. I know he likes my comic acts, and I started to perform. I resurrected jokes I'd heard in my childhood and dirty jokes listening to comedians in the clubs that I think would put him in a sexy mood. But even with all those acts that I had performed I was thinking of the beauty of the Mediterranean woman. The moment was serendipitous. Bill grabbed me. The stub hairs on his face trace their way and moved to my lips. It led to deep passion for my sex-hungry body. The twin bed was awaiting my arrival. I lifted my lips, and he lifted my body up and dropped me on the twin bed. We were noisy, shouting to each other, "I love you. I love you." He pulled me closer, and we stretched out the full length of our bodies. His damp mouth was on my breasts, and I became noisier. So many weeks had passed without Bill's perspiration on my body. Now I was bathing in it. I was telling myself I could never love a man the way I love Bill. He became extremely tired after his sterling performance and fell asleep in my arms. Then I was telling God not to let anything happen to Bill. But still my mind forced me to draw out my observations: with all I did he had no ejaculation. I will wait till tomorrow and call Frances in her wheelchair.

Daybreak. And I felt like a new woman, energized, practicing yoga with my feet pushing Bill off the bed.

"Ella Willa, after I did my duty under duress to the best of my ability last night that's how you treat me?"

"You need to do the same duty every night."

"I'm going to work today."

"Do you want me to come?"

"Stay home, make calls, and do bookkeeping."

We prepared breakfast and chatted as new lovers. I picked out his clothes and helped him dress. Bill likes when I tie a Sinatra knot and spend two minutes squeezing the knot in a perfectly, triangular shape as Pappy did when he worked in the law firm on Wall Street. He no longer ties that schoolboy knot after one overhand turn. He kissed me for two minutes, and that is why I spent two minutes tying the Sinatra knot.

"Bill, a Mr. Longmoor will be coming in today."

"How do you know that?"

"He told me he likes black women, and he is purposely coming in to buy me a red Cooper. Before he purchased the black Cooper, I told him I could give him zero financing for seventy two months, and he told me such is for starving people who are living above their means. He walked with two checkbooks from two different banks."

"Had I known that rich Scotsman was going to give you a red Cooper, I would have stayed home today. What's the *quid pro quo*?"

"My blackness, of course."

"You know the combination for my safe and that is not sufficient for you?"

I shook my head from left to right, and from right to left.

"Ella Willa, your punishment for your greed would be..."

"What! What!" I shouted.

"I will tell that black-woman lover to give the red Cooper to the Mediterranean woman."

"I am going to get dressed to leave with you. I want that red Cooper for myself." I rushed in the bedroom pretending I'm going to get dressed to leave with him, and Bill hobbled to the elevator laughing to the top of his voice.

For two weeks Gordon and Richard had not seen him. They greeted him as a champion with their peculiar handshake.

"How are things, East Ham guys?"

Gordon answered. "Your woman had a lot of customers. A man named Longmoor said last week that he hopes that black American woman would be coming in today."

"Why?"

"To buy the red Coop for someone as a gift."

"Did he tell you who is that someone?"

Richard answered. "That someone is your wife, Bill."

"She is not yet my wife."

"Don't both of you sleep on the same bed?"

"Yes."

"Then she is your wife. Bill, why did you come in today to prevent your wife from getting her premarital gift?"

They laughed as school boys who had just tricked the class bully and stuck a tail on his pants with the words, DUMB, STUPID, AND STINKER THAN A RAM GOAT.

The day was slow for business yet there was a constant flow of customers. Bill called Richard and Gordon to share the lunch I prepared. Gordon poured alcohol in a paper cup and handed it to Bill.

"I stop drinking that stuff, man," Bill said.

"When," Gordon asked.

"Couple weeks now."

"Your American wife stopped you. She probably noticed your imbalance."

"How do you know I have an imbalance?"

"I see you five days a week for the past five years.

At least, I should know something about you."

"What else you notice about me?"

"You don't indulge in sexual conversations as before. Probably the Mediterranean woman and the American woman burned you out."

"Mind your business. You can be fired! Mark you!" Bill told me everything that went on.

The phone rang, and Gordon picked up. "Good afternoon, Baxter and Dunkin Car Dealership, may I help you?"

"Give me the female salesman."

"Who's calling?"

"Longmoor."

"Let me put you on to my boss who knows everybody's work schedule." Gordon handed the phone to Bill and winked to him.

"William Baxter."

"Could you put on Miss Wilcox?"

"Today is her day off. How can I help you?"

"Would she be there tomorrow?"

"Quite likely."

"Tell her Whylee Longmoor called."

"Mr. Longmoor, do you care to leave a message for her?"

"Just tell her I called."

"I will. If you are in the neighborhood, drop in."

"Tell her tomorrow I will be there."

"Without fail, Mr. Longmoor."

The business day ended.

As Bill drove home, his first thought was about his two favorite employees' observations about him: Am I really showing signs that Gordon and Richard can notice? Is my doctor certain? Should I tell Ella Willa my true feeling? He stopped the car, had a long conversation with himself, then he drove home.

As I opened the door, he said, "Ella Willa, I am going to work tomorrow because...." He changed what he was going to say. "Ella Willa, I was smelling your Caribbean curry from the colonnade."

"I am not Caribbean."

"Sorry, my America woman."

"You know whenever I cook curry my payment is... Tell me."

"Your payment is like Meghan Markle's being invited to Sandringham for Christmas dinner with the Queen."

"I hope Markle 'does not have to bear the weight of her historical circumstances.'"

"She can no longer stick to her Caucasian Father's advice and 'draw her own box' in the corridor of Queen Elizabeth's power."

"At least she'll be adding some melanin to Royalty."

"Ella Willa, it doesn't take you a nanosecond to find an answer to anything street or royal."

"That's the Brooklyn in me."

I sensed he didn't like where I was heading. "Honey, the table is set. Let's eat."

Bill ate four chicken legs. I ate the breast. I looked at him enjoying his veggies and the way he was dirtying himself. I purposely dirtied myself. I let the breast fall on me and let my fingers dirty the top of his shirt that I was wearing.

"Girl, I will have to take off your shirt to wash it."

"When?"

"When I'm finished with the last leg."

"Whose leg?"

"The one nearest to me."

"That sounds good, sugar pup."

"What sounds better is if you go to work tomorrow Longmoor will be there to buy you the red Coop."

There was nonstop laughter. Having a man in the house who makes me laugh is a gift; and being in love with the man in the house is a baker's dozen. He is the extra buttered loaf. We showered together. Unknown to him I began researching deeply the multiple sclerosis disease, and I played with certain parts of his body to see if he would be aroused, and he was. I went naked on the twin bed singing, *You are too beautiful for one woman alone.* Bill changed the words as he came close to me and sang, You are too beautiful for Bill and Bill alone/ That's why Whylee wants to taste your honey. I geared myself for romance but he fell fast asleep after complaining about fatigue, pain in his ankle, and he is no good to anybody.

11

The telephone rang; Bill looked at the area code, and walked away somewhat fatigued. I was brushing my teeth in the bathroom and shouted, "Bill, why won't you pick up the phone?"

"The call is for you."

"You can pick it up. This is your house."

I rushed out of the bathroom, and picked up the phone. "Hello."

"Can I speak to Ella Willa Wilcox?"

"This is she."

"You lost your Brooklyn accent."

"Is that so?"

"Yes."

"How are you Judith?

"I'm fine."

"Are you calling to invite me to your and Pappy's wedding?"

"No. Pappy is sick, and he's hiding his sickness. He

didn't tell me, but I know he wants you to come home."

"He told you he wants me to come home?"

"No."

"Then how do you know that?"

"I have been living with him for three years, and I think I know lots of his habit, likes, and dislikes. He asked me to marry him, and I told him I love him, but I'm not ready to plunge into marriage."

"What are you waiting on to marry Pappy?"

"I'm waiting to get used to his strange ways."

I listened to her and stopped questioning her because I know Pappy has strange ways. I don't know why my Mother married him: For days he didn't speak to her; he didn't eat the food she cooked; worst still, he went to the basement and slept. I became silent.

"Are you there, Ella Willa?"

"Yes." I couldn't help going back and questioning her. "What strange ways Pappy has been exhibiting that you are afraid to marry him?"

"I think your Father is very sick."

"Sickness is not a strange phenomenon. If he is sick, he is sick. I think you are afraid to marry Pappy because you suspect his sickness will be long, and it will be a great burden on you. Isn't that so?"

Judith was silent, and I thought of a new way of questioning her about why she doesn't want to marry Pappy. "What is Pappy's illness?"

"Prostate cancer."

"How do you know?"

"My husband died from prostate cancer, and your Father has one of the symptoms. He gets up many times at nights to urinate."

"Do you go to the doctor with him?"

"No."

"Why?"

"He does not want me to go to the doctor with him. He says I am not his babysitter. But he always writes what Dr. Rudberg, his urologist, tells him on a piece of paper, and he puts the paper in his black jacket pocket in his closet."

"You are in the habit of searching his pockets?"

"Yes."

"Why?"

"Because I want to know what Dr. Rudberg tells him. I am clinical in my behavior. That's all. If you think I'm searching your Father's pockets because I want to find out what he owns, I am not a gold digger. Your Father has nothing that I want, only his company; and he needs my company more than I need his. I am at the brink of my patience."

"With Pappy?"

"No! With you!" She slammed down her phone.

Her insinuation was wrong. I had no such thoughts of her being a gold digger. I was happy that even with Pappy's no-good behavior she stayed with him. For sure, I couldn't tell Bianca she slammed down the phone on me. I questioned myself if I should tell Bill of Pappy's sickness. But my reasoning told me not to.

I went into the tub and all I remembered was I opened a tap. Sometime later Bill told me he came in the bathroom when he saw water seeping outside and shouted, "Ella Willa, this is cold, cold water! What's wrong?" He told me he lifted me out of the tub, wrapped me in a large towel, carried me on the king sized bed upstairs, and dried me all over. He said I was talking to myself saying, "If Pappy falls sick and Bill falls sick at the same time what should I do: Go to Pappy or go to Bill. I will tell Bianca to go and take care of Pappy. But they don't agree: One is lime; one is milk. Pappy is my blood; Bill is my true lover. I wonder if Pappy is not as bad as Judith said. Bill is hiding his sickness from me. His sickness could be worse than I imagine. Pappy is hiding his sickness from Judith. They are two fools who are lucky to have women who love them dearly."

When I came to my senses, I alone was in the bedroom and wondered why I was in bed upstairs in the middle of the day. The house looked different, but I learned in situation like this I should remain calm, and that is what I did. I consoled myself, went back and enjoyed my sleep. Someone kissed me, and I knew who it was. I bought the cologne.

"How was your day, Ella Willa?"

"Do I live here?"

"For the past three years."

"Do I pay rent?"

"June just ended, so you can pay July rental tomorrow."

Bill was shocked to see I was still under the large towel he had wrapped me in, and I could see he was questioning himself whether I had lost my memory or if I'm lucid. He is a smart man. There were so many occasions when I knew he was a smart man. When I first met him in Brooklyn I liked the way he approached me, with calmness, without an attitude, and he knew that his approach to a stranger, especially a female, should be done right. Somehow, wrapped in the towel, I deemed his present approach gross. His hand barely brushed the hairs on my vagina when he was covering my body with the towel. I shouted, "Who the hell are you? You are hurting me."

"I'm sorry Ella Willa. As long as I live, I will never hurt you."

"Then why are you so cruel to me?"

Bill sensed I was not lucid. It was late in the evening but he said, "Honey, I'm going to make breakfast for you—Eggs? Sausage? Coffee? Toast? Tea? Make your choice."

The word "choice" knitted my senses of what had been going on in my brain for the past twelve hours: That I had to make my choice in the case of sickness: Whether I should travel to take care of Pappy or stay in London to take care of Bill. I screamed for Bill, and he rushed from the kitchen. My normal senses returned.

"Ella Willa, Ella Willa, I'm here, honey."

"Hold me, Bill. Don't ever let me go." The towel left my body; he held me close; and said not a word. I felt the warmth from his body as I inhaled his cologne. It was as if the smell of his body was injecting sense and sensibility in my brain. I held his hands, rubbed them on my breasts, and the teats hardened.

"Ella Willa, do you want me to put on your sleepwear?"

"No. I want you to take off your clothes."

"I'm making your breakfast."

"Now is night. Why are you making breakfast?"

"Because you haven't eaten for the day."

"I don't want food. I want your love, nobody else's."
Slowly I felt my senses returning from that fog I was in. Bill only took off his slipper and jumped in bed. He tickled every part of my body with his fingers and toes. And, strangely, as much as I enjoyed whenever he did that to my body, I was not reacting so much so that Bill addressed it.

"Ella Willa, did you get an overseas call this morning?"

"This morning? This morning?"

"Yes; this morning. I did not pick up the call because it was a New York area code."

"Oh yes! The woman who lives with Pappy called me."

"About what?"

"To talk about Pappy's bad ways. That's all."

"And that call took so long?"

I realized I couldn't hoodwink Bill so I stopped bluffing and told him Judith was talking about Pappy's illness.

"Did you speak to your Father?"

"No."

"Is it a matter that you will have to go home to take care of him because you are his first born and his heart?"

The question stabbed me. I did not answer.

"Let me give you a piggyback to your clothes closet to find decent clothes." He ran with me on his back all over the bedroom to make me forget my sorrow.

"I wanted to find something else."

"Like what?"

"If Longmoor bought the reds for me."

"He said he will be coming in to see you tomorrow."

"Bill, I will be going in the dealership tomorrow to get my red Cooper. You can stay home and invite the Mediterranean."

Bill burst out in laughter, and rested me naked on the bed.

The night was a lovely night.

The next morning I made breakfast and prepared enough lunch that he could share with Gordon and Richard. When Bill left I called Pappy.

"Hello," Judith answered.

"How are you?"

"I am fine, Ella Willa. And how are you?"

"I am enjoying my stay in London. How is Pappy?"

"Pappy is Pappy. I was lucky yesterday."

"How?"

"He sat down with me and spoke at length about his sickness. I told him I always go into his jacket pocket and read what he writes about what Dr. Rudberg tells him, and the holistic medicine he has in mind to take."

I smiled. I took a selfie of my smile showing my joy that I could talk about what is in Pappy's jacket pocket without Judith becoming combative. I purposely left the subject for a while and said complimentary things about her. I thanked her profusely for being with Pappy for three years and taking good care of him. I sensed she knew I was purposely staying away from her going into Pappy's jacket pocket and her slamming down the phone on me. I had a new approach in my conversation.

"Judith, tell me a reason why you quarreled with Pappy?"

I interrupted her answer and said, "Do you have a nickname or a sweet name for Pappy? I will not use it when I'm talking to him."

"When he makes me happy in bed, I tell him, 'Thanks, Mr. Chinaman.'"

"What's that?"

"An aphrodisiac Trini men use."

I wanted to ask her if Pappy uses that stuff on her but that was taking my impertinence too far so I refrained from asking that question. Instead I said, "What did you find in his pocket that made you mad?"

"The name and address of a woman who supplies him with herbal stuffs for prostate cancer. I told him that shit is no good."

"And what he said?"

"It's good to try everything."

"I told him prostate cancer kills a man every eighteen minutes, and if he continues using that herbal stuff and stop going regularly to his urologist he will die soon. My husband was another fool who believed in health-foods-stores supplies more than his doctor's prescriptions. When his doctor sent him for an x-ray, his bones already had cancer. I read in notes in your Father's jacket pocket that his PSA (Prostate Specific Antigen) is bad, and he wants you to come home."

"Do you know anything about Pappy's finance?"

"Yes; he doesn't hide that from me."

I felt happy, and I use the occasion to end the conversation. "Judith, keep me informed regularly. I love you. Now let me speak to Pappy."

She called him. "Mr. Chinaman, Ella Willa's on the phone."

I burst out laughing.

Pappy and I spoke for an hour or more, and every time I asked him about his health, his reply was, "Ella Willa, it's not that bad. God is on my side."

"Pappy, do you believe in God?"

"Not the way your Mother did. Since God knows everything, whenever I pray to Him all I say is, 'As usual God.'"

I laughed aloud. "That's the first laugh I have for the morning. Stay strong, Pappy."

After I hung up I called Bianca. "How is my little sister?"

"I'm glad you called. Your future husband has a

dealership and you know the combination to his safe. I need a loan."

"How much?"

"What you can afford."

"I have a problem. I discussed it with you before but I want your input now. If Pappy and Bill fall very ill at the same time, whom should I run to?"

"Run to your man, and I will run to Pappy."

"Are you serious? Are you sure, Bianca?"

"Very serious, and very sure."

"Bianca, because of you..." I held my tears and mumbled, "My life will not be in shambles. I can run to Bill without having guilt that I'm neglecting Pappy." When I hung up the phone I cried a river and spoke to Pappy as if he were in front of me: Pappy, I know you love me more than Bianca. Bianca has told you hurtful things. Now I'm sending her to take care of you, and I will be staying to be with Bill. If you know I choose Bill, a white man, and not you, what would you say? I was a sickly child, and you took care of me when Mother died. Whatever I wanted you made sacrifice and you gave it to me. When I was in middle school you knew I changed my clothes when I left home and put on the clothes I had hidden in my book bag. But you pretended you didn't know. When you caught me kissing Dirk, you pretended you didn't see. As much as you were strict with Bianca, you were soft on me. Now in your sickness, I am turning my back on you. I posted on social media after what you did for me I am running to a white man. The comments on social media were numerous, for and against me: "Black bitch, after that cracker piss in your mouth, he will choose his race; girl, I don't know who you are, but follow your dreams. I'm married to a white man, and he is good as gold; you are like what Trump says you are—a shithole. Turncoat bitch, don't forget ingratitude is worse than witch craft." The last post was too dirty to print.

[Only yesterday my friend, Shontelle, who lives in Barbados, sent me a link of Rihanna thanking the Government and the people of Barbados for naming a street once called Westbury Road to the new name, RIHANNA DRIVE. In Rihanna's speech she advised the children to follow their dreams and to believe in God. Less than an hour later I could not believe what I heard on social media: "Rihanna told the children of Barbados 'If Jesus can't help you, go to Satan.'"] [I consoled myself saying, "Thank God, nobody on social media knows me."]

I went back putting all my thoughts on Pappy as if he's in his easy chair listening to me.

Pappy, last week Bill asked me to marry him, and he is waiting on an answer from me. What should I tell him? Have you lost your racist bone? I hope so. You slammed down the phone on Bill, and he said even if he's in a wheelchair, he'll be in your house when he asks you for permission to marry me. I told Bill if we have a son he will be called James.

The phone rang and disturbed my thoughts. "Hello."

"Honey, I hope you are dressed up for dinner tonight. I have a lady guest with me."

"One who can stay over for us to do a threesome?"

"Sure!" Bill's phone was on speaker.

"I always wanted to have that experience. In Brooklyn in the Power Room the girls told me if I didn't have that experience there'll be nothing to smile about when I'm ninety and sitting in my rocking chair."

Bill opened the door. Bianca walked in, and said, "Sorry, sis. I'm not the Mediterranean chick."

Our laughter was riotous up to the dinner table.

12

Life throughout the years has been wonderful. It was my fourth year in London. Bill's finance played a great part in representing me at Immigration for my extension. I feel happy to be legally entitled to stay. I thought everything was in my favor until the phone rang. "Hello."

"Can I speak to William Baxter?"

"Who is calling?"

"Dr. Harbough."

"William is not home."

"Is he your husband?"

"No; but he treats me as his wife."

"Tell William to call his neurologist."

"Can you tell me why?"

"If you were his wife, I'd tell you. Get married soon, madam."

"Is tomorrow too late?"

"Something like that." He hung up.

I began to think but my thoughts didn't make sense. I'm living with a man all these years, and I'm not married to him. He is rich. Nothing is wrong with him except his sex is not as good as before. But I am satisfied with what he does in bed. What he does is called evolving. I don't need what Westy did in bed anymore. Just thinking of that bastard annoys me to know that I let him treat me like dirt. He even hit me if he thought I had a man with him. I didn't tell Pappy because I knew Pappy would shoot him and go to prison, satisfied for his act. I didn't tell Bianca because I knew she'd have her gang blunt his knees. Now I have a man who loves me. My thoughts deepened. Why does Dr. Harbough want to speak to him personally? Does Bill want to give him a deal on the American cars Bill will soon be importing? Dr. Harbough could be one of the chess players Bill hangs out with. Dr. Harbough probably wants to surprise me and drop by because Bill tells him of my Caribbean-American cooking.

I told myself, in my case, when I was seriously ill and the doctor found in my x-ray things I should know, the doctor let his nurse call me, so why is Dr. Harbough calling Bill, and not his nurse. I became suspicious that Bill was very ill, and he didn't want to tell me. I went on the computer and read Multiple Sclerosis is a demy eliminating disease in which the insulating covers of nerve cells in the brain and spinal cords are damaged. Bill left for work that morning and my eyes looked at every part of his body to see if I can detect what part of his body is damaged. He showed interest and pleasure in what he did last night, and he spoke of his intention of importing American cars so I assumed there were no symptoms of a major depressive episode with him. Nonetheless, I guessed he had feelings of tiredness that Dr. Harbough was calling about. But I noticed when Bill walked to his car some gait anomalies were evident—he dropped his foot down; and he dropped his toe down. I remember when I visited Frances at Jamaica Hospital she told me that's one of the signs of MS patients. Once Bill dialed, without going to his memory pad, to get customers, now he depends on me to get phone numbers.

I stopped thinking of the reasons why Dr. Harbough called. It was better to think of fun things like Whylee Longmoor promising to buy the red Cooper for me; how he reneged on his promise; and how that would be a laughing stock for Bill when I tell him and act like a clown with him in my circus. I thought of my elementary school friend, Jim, who came 28th in test. He rubbed off the 8, left it with "2," handed his Mother his school report and boasted, "Mother, I came 2nd in class." His Mother replied, "Jim, I see you came tooth." That's how she pronounced 2th. I laughed as if Jim and I were still in grade three at PS 269.

Bianca called, and I stopped laughing.

"Ella Willa, I think I will have to go and see Pappy. The doctor is sending him to have an MRI (magnetic resonance imaging). That means the doctor thinks he has prostate cancer and wants to see if the cancer reaches his bones."

"Bianca, the other bad news is Dr. Harbough called to speak to Bill personally, and I didn't like the joke he made."

"What was it?"

"He said tomorrow is too late to marry Bill."

"Girl, that's an English joke."

"The tone in Dr. Harbough's voice said Bill is very ill."

"Ill with what?"

"I think I told you before."

"What?"

"My suspicion is Multiple Sclerosis."

"And you kept it so silently." She displayed her annoyance. "You are no different from that stupid woman who is living with Pappy."

"Bill never allowed me to accompany him to his doctor, and I tried many times to go with him."

"What made you suspect it is MS?"

"I have been speaking to my friend, Frances, who has MS and is now in a wheelchair. She told me Bill has all the early signs that she had."

"Like what?"

"His failing vision; his fatigue; he is not interested in sex anymore; he doesn't wish to hear me play the keyboard."

"Then he's really sick. I've already booked to travel on Sunday."

"Bianca, I beg you, please, be nice to Judith."

"That woman who doesn't know my name, and she

thinks I'm an untamed animal?"

"She's taking care of Pappy. Be nice to her." The color ID showed Bill is on the phone, and I switched over. "Bill, will you marry me?"

"Ella Willa, I have been asking for your hand in marriage four years now, and I've been turned down three times. What's the hurry today?"

"Dr. Harbough called to speak to you or his wife, no one else. Is something wrong with you? I suspect you are likely to be having MS. At what stage it is?"

He did not answer.

"Why did you call me, Bill?"

"To take you out to Sky Garden. It is a food experience not to be missed."

"Why not take me to Dr. Harbough and tell him I'm at liberty to sit through your examination and ask questions about the man I'm going to marry?"

"That could be arranged."

"When?"

"Tomorrow."

"I love you, honey. Please, don't disappoint me. After dining out, we will relax on the twin bed."

His laughter from the phone hit my face. It was like Santa Claus saying ho, ho, ho. Once I had asked the Mediterranean woman, how she and Bill met. She said his laughter met her after he drank beer at a neighborhood pub. She was with her husband and told her husband, "I wish you could laugh as that guy with the beer in his hand. My husband took me to him, and we introduced ourselves to him." Now I wish when I hear Bill's doctor's diagnostics tomorrow I will be laughing as loudly as the guy with the beer in hand because of good news. But good news is not always synonymous with life.

I dressed very sexy in a low-cut, cream, silk top, black pencil skirt, slit high, backless high heels, and my black body that could be seen was creamed and felt like velvet. I knew where Bill would put his finger, and I left a note for him that said, Don't forget the twin bed is my choice. When he saw me, he ran to me, squeezed me and began to cry.

"Don't cry, Bill. I love you."

"Ella Willa, forgive me for hiding my sickness. After Dr. Harbough did not get me at home, he called me at the dealership and told me to come and bring you. He felt the concern in your voice when he spoke to you."

"We hardly exchanged words, and yet he felt my concern over you?"

"Yes, he did. He detected your American English and asked, 'Who are you?' I told him I'd asked you to marry me many times, and you always turned me down."

"Bill, right now I'm only interested in hearing about your health, not whether or not you'll marry me."

"What about my business that I've spent my life building and thinking about since I was an orphan?"

"You are storing up your treasures on earth for whom?"

"Where did you learn that storing-up-treasures-on-earth line?"

"From my Christian Mother, the pastor at Divine Truth Assembly." I eased myself from his grip, wiped his eyes with the ball of my index finger, and changed the subject. "How do you like my looks for dinner?"

He smiled, and looked at me from head to toe. He put his index and middle fingers in my bra, took out the note, and laughed aloud. I was glad he was no longer sad. I took his briefcase from his hand and rested it on a chair. "Let's go, my love." I took the car keys. "I'll drive. I'll pay for dinner with my plastic. I'll pay for romance later too. And I called the Mediterranean to join us."

"For dinner only, I hope."

"You had something else in mind?"

Bill could not stop laughing. I stopped the car. "Bill, this is the last chance you have to bid to fulfill every man's dream of having two nasty and beautiful broads in bed, doing a *ménage a trois*."

He laughed louder.

"Going once, going twice...."

He shouted, "What's the price?"

"You stayed too long to answer. Sold!"

Bill laughed longer and louder than his usual Santa blueprint. We came out of the car and laughed joyously together. Drivers tooted, and asked me, "Did he bend on his knees to put the ring on your finger?"

Bill shouted, "I had an opportunity to put the ring another place but I blew it."

"What happened, Jack?" one asked.

As Bill got in the car, he shouted, "I blew it, man.

You would have liked to put it there too."

"With that nice choc-o-late, you couldn't find the way, Jack?"

Bill drove off and turned right.

"That's not the way to the Mediterranean."

"Ella Willa, I didn't know you were serious. We are now on A406 Highway, and I can't turn around."

"Coward, we were going to give you the best night in your life."

"I am a sick man, and I didn't want you two to be grading my tepid performance."

"From A to A minus is not a bad grade. I had a D in high school, yet I obtained a Master's Degree from NYU."

He looked at me and squeezed my hand. We sang a medley of songs until we reached the restaurant. As the valet drove off, I held Bill's hand and said, "I love you." We were ushered to our table.

"What would you have to drink?" the waiter asked.

"Rum and coke," I said.

"You, sir?"

"Ice tea."

My mind tells me probably the doctor told him to stay away from alcohol. I called the waiter. "Make it two ice teas."

"Ella Willa, why you did that?"

"I like whatever my man likes. He doesn't like the Mediterranean in bed the same time with me, and I'm for that too."

He looked at me, smiled, and I passed my hand on

his head. "Bill, your hair is thinning. You want some of mine?"

"From where should I pull the American's?"

I burst out laughing.

The waiter said, "Ice is in the tea. Don't let it choke your laughter." Her name was on her uniform.

"Doreen, it's the best laughter I had in months. Our dinner, please." The dinner was lavish—a wide choice of meat and fish dishes as well as excellent vegetarian options beautifully presented. I kissed Bill. "Tell me something about London that is not written in books, your boyhood included."

"From what age do I start?"

"Puberty."

"Why do you like hairs, girl?"

My laughter came without effort. Bill's too. Diners looked at us, but we didn't care. We laughed until the dinner was put before us.

The dinner was lavish without wine.

"Ella Willa, I'm very tired. You'll have to drive me home."

"Tomorrow you will have to tell Dr. Harbough about that endless tiredness."

"He already knows that. He has been giving me a prescription for it."

"I have never seen you taking any prescription, sneaky." I looked at him. "You have been depressive at times I've noticed."

"You never asked me why."

"As humans, we all have our ups-and-downs days. I'm sure you knew when I was in the doldrums, and you left me alone. For that matter, I screamed at you for still keeping Benadetta as a friend, and you didn't want me to apologize, even when I pushed all the dishes off the table with rage, left them on the floor, and you cleaned up. Would you accept my apology now?"

"Yes; by picking up the tab for this lovely six-course dinner."

"That's your money I took from the safe so that's not a good apology."

"Well, give the waiter a big tip and tell her that's for your apology."

We had finished our dinner. The waiter came. I said, "Doreen, this is for your great service." She took the money. "And this extra is for my apology." She looked at the money intently.

"I'm new on the job. Did I do something horribly wrong when I served you?"

"You did everything right to please me and my future husband."

"You chose a date?"

"No. But he will be surprising me soon."

"How soon?"

"Ask him." She looked at Bill.

Bill bowed to her. "Goodnight, Doreen. I will be calling you for tips on taming an American woman who thinks the Mediterranean woman is the competition."

"What! What!"

"Just wait on my call, Doreen."

After Bill laughed for many minutes, he went to bed as I drove home. My mind went on a wild goose chase thinking what the doctor will tell him tomorrow. After talking to Frances a week ago about how long MS took to put her in a wheelchair, and she told me exactly three years, the first question I told myself that I would ask the doctor is: Could I handle the task of pushing my husband in a wheelchair and continue to run his dealership? He has never told me his background—whether he has or had parents or siblings. I had told Bill repeatedly of my background with the hope he'd say something about his, but to no avail. I asked myself whom should I employ to help me when Bill becomes very sick. Then as much as I condemned Pappy's prejudicial ways, I knew I must be converse to his ways by choosing people with the know-how about cars and the business sense of running a dealership, regardless of their color, race, religion, or ethnicity, not limiting my choice for people from only London or Norway but also people from wherever they live on earth to help me run the business of Baxter and Dunkin Car Dealership.

I stopped and looked at the view below, our favorite view showing the spine of London with its twisting highways. This is the spot where Bill first made love to me in the car. This is the spot where he said, "Ella Willa, you are like good wine, and good wine needs no bush." I told him, "William Baxter, the dynamic between you and me is very interesting."

"Like what, Ella Willa?"

"You said I'm like good wine. Why not drink me out of the bottle?"

"Where is the bottle?"

"Your hand is touching it."

"Are you objecting?"

"Of course not!"

As the memories mounted like heaps of sea sand on me in the Atlantic Ocean down at Coney Island on a hot day in summer, I went closer to him and hugged him. I felt his heart beat and whispered in his ear, and not expecting him to answer, I said, "Where do you feel weak when I'm close to you—any specific place, or all over?"

Faintly, he said, "Ella Willa, what did you say?"

"Bill, I'm so sorry for waking you up."

"Where are we?"

"The place where you first touched my pearl."

"On the bed?"

"No. At the lookout."

He smiled.

His smile lit my whole body. If I didn't have to drive him home safely, I would have stripped myself to mark the memory. I obeyed sanity and drove home singing Pappy's favorite Kitty Kallen's rendition. *Little Things Mean a Lot.*

As we walked into the elevator, Bill said, "What do you want us to do tonight?"

"Whatever you wish, hon."

"I want to be molested by you because tomorrow

my doctor may say stay away from that American broad."

"Why would he say such a thing?" He was thinking of an answer, and I said, "Let's play cards."

"In bed?"

"No. You cheat whenever we play cards in bed." I changed my card game suggestion and said, "You think Dr. Harbough will want you to give up your business?"

"If he does, you can run it. I want to see your Pappy before I get worse. I want to go to him and tell him I want his permission to marry you."

I was too shocked to answer. "Bill, tea or coffee?"

"Tea for two like Doris Day."

"You want me to play it?"

"Sure."

"Boogey style?"

"Yep."

He sat by me; I played; and he imitated Satchmo. I took off my clothes, changed into a long nightgown, knelt, and prayed softly to God in earnest. We went upstairs on the king-sized bed, and he slept in my arms. I wished there was a crystal ball that tells the story of William Baxter's life in the future.

13

I had an uncomfortable chair in the examination room as if it were meant for me to be uncomfortable. The nurse told me to sit. Dr. Harbough rested his stethoscope on his neck and introduced himself. He was quite affable, but he shocked me when he said, "You people in America have a moron in the White House, and the Republicans let that yellow-haired racist slide as slime under their feet." He saw the stunned look on my face, and he ended his politics. "How do you like London, Miss Wilcox?" I told him I like London very much, but I love Bill more, and soon he'll be my husband when you can tell me more about him. He said I look nervous. He playfully took the stethoscope from around his neck, put it barely on my chest as if he were afraid I would complain about him touching me, and said, "Miss America, you are okay."

I smiled. "Doctor, I know I am not yet married to Bill, but can you tell me about Bill's past examinations and what you will be doing on Bill today?" I purposely repeated that statement of not being Bill's wife.

"Ms. Wilcox, if William Baxter says it is okay with him, it's okay with me." He looked at Bill who nodded affirmatively.

He looked at me, and I said, "Dr. Harbough, call me Ella Willa."

"Ella Willa, I love when a patient's caregiver asks questions. I am going to do first the OCT (Optical Coherence Tomography) which measures the thinning of the retina. I cannot tell you the result right away."

"I understand." I felt so comfortable that I did not question him again on whatever he did. I just looked on as he asked Bill questions and placed the stethoscope over different parts of Bill's body. He had Bill stand on one foot; then walk in a straight line. He told Bill the OCT technique has the potential to provide a powerful and reliable assessment strategy to measure structural changes in the central nervous system. He checked Bill's muscle strength, reflexes, coordination, and asked Bill if he suffers from dizziness. Bill said yes.

"Bill, I am going to ask you about your private life. Do you want Ella Willa to leave the room?" Dr. Harbough looked at Bill.

"No."

"Give me the history background of your life—parents, siblings, as far back as you remember. I want to trace their DNA."

"I know nothing of them. I grew up in a home and was told nothing about who I am."

"You ever inquired to know?"

"Never."

I put my head down. My eyes began to flood.

Dr. Harbough asked him, "Is your sex life okay?"

"Not as before."

"Meaning?"

"I don't get an erection, and no ejaculation."

"Does Ella Willa complain?"

"Never! She does as if I'm Mandingo, and I feel happy when she screams."

Dr. Harbough could no longer stifle his laughter.

Dr. Harbough looked at me, and I whispered, "Yes." I changed the subject. "Dr. Harbough, my friend who has MS is now in a wheelchair. She told me that came after three years. How many years Bill's sickness will put him in a wheelchair?"

He delayed answering me, and said, "He may never be in a wheelchair."

Bill said, "Doctor, my fatigue does not go away even when I rest."

"Do you take your prescriptions the same time every day? I have an idea you don't take them as prescribed. Ella Willa, you take charge of his meds now."

I looked at Bill and he knew why. "Dr. Harbough, I'm going in the waiting room."

"Okay, Ella Willa. I will spend about half an hour more with Bill. There's hot tea outside. You can come back whenever you wish."

He kept Bill for another hour. In speaking with his

nurse, she told me there's no known cure for the disease, "but your husband will be fine with medical management. I've seen other MS patients who have improved. Your friend who is in the wheelchair could be in it because of other illnesses."

She poured me another cup of tea and asked, "Are you American?"

"Yes; from Brooklyn."

"I have a T-shirt from Brooklyn which reads, F--K QUEENS. What's wrong with Queens?"

"Nothing. People from Brooklyn are imaginative. That's all."

After an hour, Dr. Harbough called me to come in his office. "Ella Willa, here are his prescriptions. Remember you are in charge. Do not let him drive home." Then he whispered in my ear. "He has those two words, MS. And it is above the beginning stage. I'll see him in two weeks."

As we walked to the car, I asked, "Who's driving home, Bill?"

"You, Mother."

"Mother has your prescriptions. Son, I will put you on my lap and spank you if you don't obey Mother."

"Mother, I will obey you as if I'm in kindergarten."

"Bill, I've read there are thirty six million people with disabilities in the United States and..." I didn't end the sentence.

"If I become one, chronic, would you be gone?"

"Bill, you are the best thing that ever happened to me. I've told you this, and I mean it. Pappy is ill, and as much as he wants me to come home, I will not. I have suspected your silence meant you are hiding your sickness. If you end up in a wheelchair, I will be pushing you. Nobody else! Have you tried to find out who are your parents to know something about their DNA?"

"No."

"Why?"

"I grew up in a house with other children just as I not knowing anything about our background. But there was Theodosius. If God created one child in the world with His hands, it was Theo, the man child. God made this man child a sociologist who believes life should be a liberating experience. Theo behaved as if we, the inmates of the home, are his world from which he elicits the *pros* and *cons* of life. I used to mope thinking of the day I'll see my Mother bringing my brothers and sisters to meet me; and they will be coming in a big, big car driven by my Father to take me home with them in their gigantic house. It was as if Theo read my thoughts one day, or probably God told him to talk to me with the wisdom He, God, has given Theo: 'Bill, I'm so happy I don't have brothers and sisters. I can tell myself how to think, how to dream, and how to behave so the future will be what I want it to be.'" The conversation continued.

"Theo, what you want to be in the future?" I had asked as we sat on the stoop of the building that the landlord often chased us off.

"Bill, I want to own a dealership." He was nine years old.

"What is a dealership, Theo?"

"A big, big house filled with plenty cars, and I will sell each car cheaper than everybody else."

"Where would you find those cars to sell?"

"From my imagination."

"Theo, I'm going to do just as you and join your company and stop my crying for people who don't want to see me. And when I get rich in a dealership like yours and those people who never knew me come to know me to get money, I will tell them to go to their imagination to see how I got my money. And if they come to me and tell me their imagination did not give them money, I will tell them to contact you because you are the genius who taught me everything."

I stopped Bill from telling me his flash-back story because I saw he was tired and emotional. He stopped speaking and quickly fell asleep. I drove into the garage, woke him up, and held his arm firmly to the elevator.

After dinner, I called Pappy, and Bianca picked up.

"Hi, Ella Willa."

"Bianca, bad news. My suspicion about Bill having multiple sclerosis is true. His doctor told me his MS has passed the beginning stage. His balance is very bad, and I run the business. Bill knew something was going wrong with his body, and he taught me the business very early. I was wondering why he spent so much time pounding into my brain techniques of sale and telling me in business there is no friendship when you are losing. At times I was annoyed, and when I told him to give me a break, he said in business there is no break when the competition is ready to cut your throat. Now I am an astute business-man. My business acumen is second to none. Nobody can cut my f--kin throat, only if I let them."

"I never told you this: Before you came to London, Bill and I hanged out in bars, in clubs, and in seedy places where everybody congregates and talks bullshit. Sometimes Bill suddenly lost interest in our activity. Another time he got very weak, and I had to drive him home. I'd asked him if he's suffering from depression because of the pressure to stay ahead in the business. He answered me and said, 'I hope one day I'd have someone who is honest to help me.' I told him you will fill that gap because of your sterling character and honesty. After you told me about him, and you gave me his address and phone number, I researched his life. I could not find anything about his background but luck came my way, and a friend told me about his dealership. Every time I had spoken to him, he had asked me, 'When is Ella Willa coming to London?'"

I wanted to continue hearing about Bill's interest in me, but it was time for me to ask about Pappy. "How is Pappy getting on?"

"I took him to Dr. Rudberg, and he has a date for his procedure in Brighton Beach, Brooklyn."

"How are you and Judith getting on these days?"

"Very well. Her bark is worse than her bite. There's another thing that I never told you about Bill."

"What?"

"When Bill was sure you were coming to London,

he told me he ended his close relationships with all his women because he fell in love with you from the time he saw you."

"Sister, because of you I have the man I truly love, in sickness and in health. In three years, more or less, his nerve cells in his brain and spinal cord could be badly damaged. I may have to push him in a wheelchair."

Bianca became silent. I could hear her breath coming through the phone.

I hung up, and collected Bill's meds. "Bill, Mother is bringing your meds in the bathroom. Can Mother come in?"

"What are the names of those meds?"

"I can't pronounce those names. Are you naked?"

"No. You don't even want to see me naked even on the twin bed?"

"I'll give that a thought after you come out of the tub, and I can go in." He came out.

I went in the tub and soaked my body to the tune of Miles Davis playing 'Round Midnight. The bubble bath covered my whole body. I felt like calling Bill to join me but changed my mind. In times like these I feel like writing my autobiography. But what would I put in it? Surely, not how Westy used to beat me up. Not how I slapped the glass from Benadetta's hand. Not how I stole candy in the bodega when I was in kindergarten. Probably I'd write about the first time I had sex and how I enjoyed it so unlike what a woman on Wendy Williams Show said: She's in love with a pastor; she needs sex; and the pastor is saying he will not have sex until they are married. In my autobiography I will expand on the power of sex, and if I had a pastor who didn't want sex before marriage I'd tell him to leave me alone and go looking for Sister Theresa.

The temperature in the tub was just right, and I stayed longer than I'd intended. When I stepped out of the tub, I could not stop that happy feeling and told myself I would do whatever Bill wants me to do on the twin bed. I walked naked into the room. Bill was sound asleep. I put his head in my arms, saw his hair thinned more, and said, "I will be around, honey, when the last strand falls." I didn't know when I too fell asleep, neither did I remember my happy dream. But I awoke, lucid, with the man I love making love to me.

14

Bianca called. "Are you celebrating on Sunday?"

"Celebrating what?"

"Your fourth anniversary of meeting Bill."

"What's the big deal?"

"Bill is sick. Make him feel happy to know that you care. You don't have to buy a car for him. You can tell Whylee Longmoor to send your car to him." We laughed.

"I am not going to tell you anything about my personal life again."

"And I am not going to tell you what Pappy and Judith are thinking of doing."

"Please, please, tell me, my loving baby sister."

"They are thinking of getting married. You and Bill should do the same."

"Bill has asked me to marry him, and I've turned him down so many times. The next time he proposes, I'll tell him to do it in front of Pappy. Don't you think that's a great idea, especially if we get married in Brooklyn, and we have a double wedding?"

"Big sister, that's the best suggestion you made since kindergarten."

"You are five years under me, and you know nothing of my kindergarten years at PS 269."

"I knew when you kissed Jimmy in the backyard, and he asked you to feel his hard penis."

"But I didn't feel it. But you cut classes to go to movie with that Russian boy—what's his name again?"

"I don't know who you talking about."

"The pale looking boy from Brighton Beach who wore the same clothes every week."

"I still don't know who you talking about."

"I don't believe you. Let's get back to having a double wedding. Do you think my idea is good?"

"If you can get Bill to come."

"I will work on that, but my priority is his health."

"Don't forget to celebrate on Sunday your fourth anniversary together, and tell him you are ready to accept his proposal."

"Because of you, Sister...."

"Ella Willa, this time it is because of you." She hung up.

I took the three prescriptions in my hand with a glass of water and woke Bill up. "Honey, your doctor says to have your meds the same time every day."

"Okay, Mother."

My mouth opened to say, Was your Mother a black woman, but my commonsense said, "Honey, I love when you call me Mother."

"Why?"

"Mothers love their first born; and you are my first born in true love. You are the man I prayed for in my dreams—a man of substance, not of straw. When you are asleep I pray to God to heal you. I prayed to God to ask you to marry me."

"You didn't have to pray to God. I'd asked you to marry me before and you turned me down countless times. Today I'm asking you: Would you marry me in Brooklyn if I propose to you in front of Pappy?"

The glass dropped from my hand and smashed.

"Does that smash mean yes?"

He was sitting on the edge of the bed. I threw my reduced weight of one hundred and twenty one pounds on him and shouted, "Yes! Yes! Yes!"

"I will call Gordon and Richard and tell them you said yes. They always tease me telling me you will never marry me because only Brooklyn and the boys in the hood are your true love. Now I'll tell them I'm going to marry you in Brooklyn because there is where we found each other. Today we go ring shopping. I know you are frugal like hell. Don't choose anything cheap. What did you just tell me?"

"Yes! Yes! Yes! Marry me, Ella Willa Wilcox."

"I'm taking you to Daniel Prince, one of the best jewelers in London."

Bill's memory of our meeting in Brooklyn and what we spoke about surpassed mine. His excitement of marrying me made me happy. The morning's air made Bill's words more genuine. I hugged him and used words of love that flowed from my heart. His lips were close to mine, and I let the fire start by rubbing my nipples on his chest which was my trademark. I hadn't sex in a month. I dreamed of having rough sex, and meant to put him in the mood.

"I want to get jealous, Bill. Tell me about you and the Mediterranean in bed. Tell me what she did to you, and how you liked it."

"I had told her about you, and she wasn't jealous. All she said was when you come to London three of us will be in bed."

"And why you refused to do it when I asked you?"

"Because you satisfy me as nobody did."

I did not expect the morning to be flesh on flesh. He tugged gently the strings that held my top together until the top was undone and my bra was loose. The exotic intensity that was piled within me made me so erratic that I forgot Bill was a sick man suffering from dizziness, muscle weakness, fatigue, and pain in his ankle. Needing sex made me selfish and thoughtless. I forgot he needed to enjoy the moment too as when we first met. In those days I let him know all the positions I like, and he told me he'd never forget them. And he never did. Now I was cruel in my love making. I forgot the pain in his knee when I propped them. When he panted I forgot he suffered from fatigue and only thought he was enjoying my cruelty with deep groans. I stopped when he said, "That's enough. I'm in pain."

I rolled off him. He never spoke again, and I was concerned. I hugged him. I blew in his face. And I prayed. "Lord, don't let him die."

He whispered, "I almost."

"Am so sorry, honey. This is a day in the life of a fool—me."

"Don't blame yourself. Blame me too. I could have said no from the beginning but I thought I had the stamina."

We smiled thinking what could have happened.

He asked for a Caribbean breakfast, and I prepared it my Mother's style: toast, eggs scrambled in salted fish with onions, bake, fried fish, tea, orange juice, and fruits. I fed him, and he fed me. We talked; we laughed; we resurrected childhood jokes; and he begged me to repeat the joke in Trini lingo of Pappy being booed off the stage in the talent show when he sang *Fools' Paradise.*

"Ella Willa, tell me again what the crowd told Pappy in their Fyzabad twang, please."

"Leh (let) we chook him down with ah gullet as if we chookin down cocoa off ah tree. He's no f--kin good."

We laughed, walked to the tub, and played as children in the water.

We went and bought the rings at Daniel Prince, but he would not let me see the price when the clerk returned his debit card and receipt. He put the rings in his pocket, destroyed the receipt, and I never saw neither the engagement ring nor the wedding ring again.

Bianca called to say Pappy had a successful prostate procedure, and he is recuperating nicely with pain killers.

Life went on as usual. Sometimes Bill went to work, and when he felt fatigued and could not travel, I went to work. I love the job of selling cars. I met customers who wanted to know more about who I am than which car they are interested in buying. I get the sense that English people are polite and inquisitive but not friendly.

I was early at work. Whylee Longmoor walked in. I stretched my hand. "I'm so happy to see you."

"Where have you been? You went back to the moron who wants to bomb North Korea?"

"Who is that?"

"You are not following U.S. politics?"

"Not lately."

"I heard the big man in the White House intends to end health care for the poor and cut taxes for the rich which makes sense. Being poor, if you were still there you would have suffered. But you are doing well in this country."

"Tell me more of your unguarded insolence, Mr. Longmoor. I see you hate people like me coming here."

He looked at his watch. "I have to go."

"It gives me great pleasure to see you go. Mr. Showoff, when are you going to stop beating your wife?"

Gordon and Richards were listening to our conversation and as Longmoor stepped out of the dealership, they shouted in unison, "You f--kin racist. You will need air in your flat tires, and we are closed."

Those two employees protected me night and day. Sometimes they pretended they were strangers when shady characters came in the dealership. One day I asked, "Which one of you loves me more?" No one answered.

"Because neither of you loves this American woman, I am not inviting you to my wedding."

"When?" they shouted.

"If you love me, I'll tell you when."

They looked at each other. Gordon said, "Where?"

"In Brooklyn."

"How do I get there?" Richard asked.

"First, get a passport."

"How soon?"

"In one month's time."

"Are you kidding? You don't have an engagement ring."

"Bill will be in tomorrow. Ask him, and he'll tell you why I'm not wearing an engagement band. He'll also tell you if you decide to come, he will cover your expenses."

They shouted, "Is that true?"

"Yes; that's true."

"How is his health?" Gordon asked.

"Healthy enough to get married to the woman he loves."

Gordon looked in my eyes and asked, "If the day comes when he is too weak to come to work, would he sell the business?"

"If that day comes he will compensate both of you

justly."

"Ella Willa, why not tell him you can run the business. We will be just as faithful to you. You had promised to bring a keyboard in the dealership. When would you bring it? I heard you tickle those black and white keys and put Bill to bed."

"He told you so?"

"Yes," they said.

I looked at them. They laughed hiding their teeth.

Gordon said, "the blacker the berry, the sweeter the juice."

I pretended I did not hear what Gordon said. "Time to close, guys." I stifled my laughter.

On my way home, I hummed *Harlem Nocturne* as if Larry Elgart's band were background music. I always liked Harlem. Pappy used to take me to Jazz Mobile there, and I met many of the jazz greats. I liked Dizzy Gillespie best. I knew Harlem in two stages—when most of the brownstones were dilapidated, cheap on the market, and men and women were shooting needles in their arms. Now the poor people are priced out with rich gentrification. That's what money does when money walks in. As I passed the lookout I giggled to know what a difference a day makes. Bill doesn't stop here again to bet what color panty I'm wearing and wins. He always peeped to see what panty I'm putting on. What a caring guy who hadn't a Father or Mother to take their example, or siblings to learn to share an apple with them. Yet his life is exemplary. I had asked him why he had searched my purse and read the letter Westy wrote me before I came to London. He said I talked in my sleep and couldn't believe what Westy did to me. I believed him. He doesn't lie.

When I put my key in the door and opened it, I smelled dinner. It was burning. I took off the stove and rushed in the bedroom. "What's wrong, Bill?"

"I don't know. My muscles collapsed."

"Did you take your medicine?"

"Bring it for me."

I rushed for them, put them individually in his mouth, and gave him water to swallow them. "Bill, when this pain started?"

"When I started to cook for you."

"Honey, don't ever cook for me again. I will do the cooking. Furthermore, I will cook before I leave in the morning." I kissed him, held his hand, and put him in the loveseat.

"Sorry, Ella Willa, that I didn't finish our dinner."

"What you cooked is enough. That last pot is *lagniappe* which was not necessary."

"Medicine has funny names. Now what's that funny name, *lagniappe*?"

"It's like a baker's dozen, something extra. My parents always use that word. I hear people in New Orleans use that word too."

"It's like bringing the Mediterranean in bed?"

"You are good with your similes? What's your grammar teacher's name? I want to talk to her."

"Are you thinking of switching the young Mediterranean for old Maggie?"

"I want to ask her if she's the one who is instrumental for your business acumen."

"And if she tells you no?"

"I'll ask her about your behavior in class."

"I called Dr. Harbough. He said I can come in tomorrow. Would you drive me?"

"That question was unnecessary. I will be with you for the rest of my life."

"I will ask the doctor for one-month's prescription to take to Brooklyn."

I looked at him. "Why one-month's?"

"When I marry the girl of my dreams I'll want to stay a little in a nice hotel to see New York. I'm not the guy who saves money for the rainy days. Any day, rainy or not, is just as good. That was the motto I learned from Theodosius Dunkin.

We had dinner.

"Bill, the burnt *lagniappe* was delicious."

"So you like my burnt egg plants."

"I want a repeat. You should have this dish patented."

He laughed Santa style. "Tomorrow I will ask Dr. Harbough if he knows the wonderful work Watson is doing in medicine."

"Who is he?"

"He is the A.I. (artificial information) guy. Watson is extending people's lives; he seeks and finds complaints that doctors are unable to find in humans. I will want

Watson to cure me. He is a comprehensive tool. If I die from MS I will want my body for experiment by Watson."

I was getting too sad to say a word.

"Are you listening to me, Ella Willa?" He raised his voice.

"Yes, I'm listening, Bill. If science can use me as an experiment to cure you, I will give myself to science."

"You don't really mean that?"

"What do you want me to do to prove that?" I raised my voice higher than his, and I looked at him as an angry bull. "Whenever you have doubts about the way I love you, ask Bianca. It is because of you I am in this country for this length of time. My Father had prostate cancer, and I sent her to take care of him. And I'm here happily taking care of you—not for your money, not for your big house in this ninety nine percent Caucasian-people neighborhood, not for your dealerships, but for you. Of late you are making remarks that irk me to my bones. Last week you said—I better not say it."

"What I said?"

"I am not going to say it." I ran upstairs, slammed the door, and locked it. I cried aloud, and trembled when I cried. I assumed he would have come upstairs, knocked, and I would have opened the door to get his apology. No such thing. My only thought was to go downstairs and put the wares in the dishwasher after I dried my tears. I always walk with my cell in my pocket. I took it out and called Bianca.

"Hi, Ella Willa. You never called me this time of the

day. What's wrong?"

"I just feel like calling my little sister."

"The pitch of your voice has a sad tone. Spill it, sister. I'm younger but I know everything about your ways, especially when you are lying. What's wrong?"

"Bill is not himself these days."

"His sickness is getting you down?"

"Yes."

"What his doctor said?"

"I'm taking him to the doctor tomorrow. He got up talking about Watson, an artificial intelligence computer. He doesn't believe his doctor is smart as Watson, and he believes only Watson can cure him." Bianca believed me, and I was happy that I didn't have to tell her the truth—Bill's disdain for me.

"Give Bill the phone. I want to talk to him."

"He's resting."

"Wake him up!"

I remained silently in the room and pretended Bill was in the same room. "Bill, wake up. Bianca wants to speak to you." I repeated myself. "Honey, wake up; your sister-in-law wants to speak to you."

"Ella Willa, leave him alone. When he wakes up tell him I love him."

Bill knocked the door as if he had a hammer in hand. I cut Bianca off before she could hear Bill's heavy knocks.

"What do you want, Mr. Baxter?"

"Please, open the door. I've come to tell you I washed the dishes, took them out of the dishwasher, dried them, put them away, and I mopped the kitchen sparklingly clean."

I opened the door. "You are not supposed to do so much in an evening, especially pushing that heavy mop."

"I did all those things to punish myself for my bad behavior to you." He bent his head and walked towards me. I was sitting upright in his favorite easy chair. I shifted, and he sat next to me. He held my left hand and said, "Can you hold my other hand, Ella Willa?"

I did, but I looked away. He pulled me into him, hugged me, and spoke in my ear. "Ella Willa, I don't know what's happening to me these days. I find myself saying things, and when I try to remember what I said in order that I may tell the doctor I can't remember. I knew when this memory problem first started, and I pretended it was just a passing phase, but now I know I have a problem. And I believe I tell you hurtful things thinking I'm talking to an enemy. Then I ask myself what did I say?" He looked at me, and I could see he was wondering if in any way he had spoken unkind words to me.

I broke his thoughts. "Honey, when you marry me, your love would always be fresh for me without a thought for the Mediterranean?"

He couldn't stop laughing. I joined him, led him to the bed, and said, "Just think of her now that you are doing it with me."

"Think both of you are doing it?"

"Yes."

Our laughter was riotous.

15

I began to relive my childhood in my mind: Our parents moved into a new neighborhood and we were the only black family on the block. Bianca and I were both born in Brooklyn Hospital and growing up on the block and attending Midwood schools I had many white friends. But Becky was my best friend, and we attended the same grade school, PS 269. At recess we rushed to the swing, and I'd push her and go to my swing and push myself. Somehow, I felt I should not let her push me.

"Ella Willa, why don't you let me push you?"

"Becky, because I'm fat, and you are not."

"If I get fat, would you let me push you?"

"If you get fat tomorrow, sure!"

"I will eat all my breakfast in the lunchroom and some of yours."

"Becky, you can't get fat in one day."

"You will see."

The bell rang and we rushed back in school hugging

each other till we walked into the class. The next morning I waited at the swing for Becky, and she never came. From Tuesday to Thursday I was on the swing by myself. On Friday I went to Miss Baker and asked her if she knew why Becky did not come to school.

"Sit down, Ella Willa."

I sat. Even at six I could sense the news I was about to get would not be good news about my friend. "Miss Baker, what's wrong with Becky? I waited for her three mornings by the swing and she did not come." I could see Miss Baker was using crutch words to kill time and thinking of the best way she should break the news to me.

She bent her head. "Ella Willa, Becky had an accident."

"When? When?"

"Last Tuesday."

"What kind of accident?"

"Someone had a DUI."

"What's that?"

"When someone drives his car drunk under the influence of alcohol. She was killed by a drunken youth who had stolen his father's car."

Going to PS 269 meant nothing to me again. I never went on the swing. I never made friends until I met Dunston. He was about to have a snow cone from the Hispanic vendor in front of the school but he allowed me to go before him. "Thank you," I said.

"I can take the place of Becky Sills and go swinging with you every morning before the bell rings."

"You know Becky?"

"She was my sister. She spoke of you every night before she went to bed. Even when she was dying, she asked for you."

I was glad when my flashback ended.

The feeling I began getting of Bill was like coming from the dealership one evening and getting news that the blow of MS has killed him. Hubris comes in many forms but when it comes in the likeness of outsmarting death—not death to prejudice, death to hatred, or death to racism—but to the death to a soul like Bill's, I'd curse death to go away. But death is inevitable. Yet one can't get used to its inevitability.

My dreams were plagued with nonsensical happenings: A dog bit me; a shark almost swallowed me; a drunk driver knocked me off the road. I hated sleeping. I'd put Bill in my arms after he had his last meds and we'd sing *Try a Little Tenderness.* He'd whisper in my ear, "Ella Willa, you are the best." I'd linger in his ear, "We are the rainbow connection—black me, white you, add the new colors."

He'd fall asleep first with his hands all over me. And I never had bad dreams again.

He began using his walker. In the doctor's office, I looked at the diplomas on the wall and thought of Bianca's pessimism: Ella Willa, some of those diplomas are bought. I sat in class with a guy at college who didn't know a hoot, and I ran into him at a hospital. He was wearing a stethoscope around his neck. For sure, he's going to be responsible for someone's death one day.

Dr. Harbough broke my thought.

"When are you two going to get married?"

Bill answered. "I bought the diamond at Daniel Prince yesterday."

"They are very, very expensive. What's the cut?"

"That's a secret."

"Am I invited?"

"If you'd come to Brooklyn, New York."

"Too far."

Bill was thoroughly examined.

"Young man, are you taking your meds on time?"

"Mother makes sure. She wakes me up to have my meds even when I'm enjoying wet dreams."

Dr. Harbough laughed; I didn't. If I'd laughed, it would have been scandalous laughter with my saying, Who's the lucky girl who gets the juice? Somehow he changed the subject and became cerebral when he opened Bill's thick folder. I said to myself, Bill can only have such a heavy folder because he had been seeking his doctor's advice long before he knew me. I'm sure the Mediterranean woman knows of Bill's sickness.

"Ella Willa," Dr. Harbough addressed me, "does Bill talk to you freely about his feelings—his ups and downs?"

"No. I have to drag it out of him."

"What he says when you drag it out of him?"

"Most times he's evasive, and he says, I wish I knew my parents to trace my DNA. I'd tell him why not try to track them down. He'd just look at me and his looks would shut me down. When I hug him he'd push me away. Whenever I tell him I'll give my life for him, he looks at me with a blank stare."

"Ella Willa, it is because he can't think straight. When multiple sclerosis begins to show its ugly head that's what happens."

I was shocked to hear the words multiple sclerosis. The doctor noticed the expression on my face, and he said, "With MS, a wife bears her husband's burdens, *vice versa*." My woman's intuition had already told me that. I said, "Doctor, what strategies will help Bill deal with his emotions?"

"Other wives have asked me that question. They tell me their husbands with businesses suffer from anxiety, fear, and frustration that they'd lose their businesses that they took years to build."

"Bill feels the same way. He thinks I can't handle his business. At present I do the export-import-bank transactions. I'm a sociologist by education. I was trained in urban planning and social management and I can adapt and be the best salesman to bring money into his business because "sociological thinking is vital to self-determination."

He stopped me. "Feeling emotional is normal when faced with a chronic illness, but your husband-to-be is not chronic." He looked at me and said, "I'd like you to leave the room now. I want to speak to him in your absence."

I kissed Bill, left the room, poured myself a cup of

tea, another, and a third. Forty five minutes later, I pushed Bill's walker in; he pushed it out to the car, stopped, kissed me, and said, "Ella Willa, my love for you will always be clear as the first dewdrops of the morning."

"Bill, mine will be mixed with rain to wash our fears away."

16

The phone rang. I picked up quickly.

"Ella Willa, Pappy is asking for you every day. When are you coming home?"

"How did his procedure go?"

"He had a radical prosectomy, and he feels I should not be the one here with him. How soon you'd be coming home?"

I thought a little, then shouted, "June first."

"Don't put off that date because Pappy and Judith are planning to marry in June, and I want you and Bill to join them."

"Bill uses a walker now. He told me he wants to propose in front of Pappy. I told him no such thing, but he insisted in proposing to me pushing his walker in front of Pappy. I told him his walker would be my arms."

"What did he say?"

"Whenever I tell him something that he doesn't like to do, but he does it nonetheless to please me, he says, 'Mother, I agree.'"

Bianca laughed, and laughed. "So you are his Mother. That's very incestuous. You still do it on the twin bed?"

"I'm not going to talk about my bedroom life."

"Do you want me to tell Westy when you are coming?"

"Hell, no!"

"Lou?"

"Neither."

"So Mother, you intend to be a-one-man woman for the rest of your life?"

"That's what it will be."

"Since June first is the date you will be on American soil, I will travel back to London next week so that both of us and Bill can travel back to New York together before June first."

"That makes sense." I hung up, and felt happy to have a little sister who can put me right.

Bill and I went to work. The staff was happy to see us. Bill used his walker to enter the dealership, but he never used it again until the day was over. He sat at his desk and conducted business. I was the salesman introducing myself and talking about cars but final negotiations were done by Bill. Many customers told me they like my accent and asked me if I'm American. Having said yes, a man introduced himself.

"I am Bristol."

"I am Ella Willa."

"It seems America wants to go it alone: Trump didn't join the Paris Accord; he was slow to say yes to NATO; he hates Muslims; and he's building a wall to block off Mexico from his Trump Towers in Manhattan." He lowered his voice, and said, "Did you read Michael Wolff's book, *Fire and Fury*? The author writes Trump's aides say Trump is like a child; he needs immediate gratification, and he does not listen. What do you think about Trump?"

"Bristol, if you buy the Clubman, I'll tell you what I may think; if you buy the black like me Countryman, I'll tell you what I should think."

He walked away, went to Bill, and completed the sale.

I said to myself Bristol thought I don't deserve the commission. The white man should give the white man the sale, not the maid. With expletives coming out of my mouth like fire, I rushed to Bill sitting at his desk.

"Ella Willa, stop absorbing that maid nonsense from white people. I absorbed their shit when I was a-nobody in the orphanage. I don't want you to think anybody is better than you. I have sufficient money to keep us going until I die. You are so f--kin cheap; you call it frugal. You said when we get married, you are not going to have a wedding to feed the whole borough—only family members and close friends. Do you want to save the money to marry Westy when I die?"

"What the f--k you just said, Bill?"

"You heard me."

I started breaking dishes, glasses, and everything that was valuable within reach. I raised my hand to punch the window of a convertible mini coop. He held my hand;

I pulled my hand, and walked and smashed the window.

"What are you doing, woman?"

"I don't want Westy to own these things when I die."

"I am sick, not you."

"Bill, you are my life, and I'll give my life as a sacrifice for your health." I told Gordon and Richard to close, and I'm taking Bill home.

Bill's walker was not close to him. He hopped to me and said, "Honey, I apologize. I'll never say what I just said again." He kept talking as I drove him home. "I will close this dealership for a month. I will pay all my employees. Before we leave to marry in Brooklyn, I will take out a life insurance policy, and you will be the beneficiary. I will put you on all my bank accounts, and the safe numbers will be changed to the date of your birth."

I wanted to ask him why, but I refrained. He was already giving me too much of his assets before marriage. Since Bianca was back from Brooklyn after Pappy felt much better, I knew I would find the time to discuss Bill's philanthropy with her. I stopped the car, kissed him, and said, "My love, I'm taking you for dinner tonight."

"Can you invite Bianca too?" he said.

"And what about the Mediterranean?" I knew that would crack him up, and I went for it.

"Get me my walker, girl. I want to go outside and dance."

"Are you going to dance because the Mediterranean is coming?"

He laughed aloud and warned me: "Please, don't

make the mistake and call her The Mediterranean when we are with strangers. Remember her name is Benadetta. If you invite her, you will have to invite her husband, Charles. Then you will have to find a companion for Bianca."

"That's no problem. Bianca has a man named Edward."

"I'm glad for the occasion because I want Benadetta to know, finally, that you will be my wife, and I love you more than anything else in the world. I also want Charles to know by my behavior during dinner that I am an honorable man."

"If Charles says, 'I'm happy, Bill, that you are going to get married because my wife would have only me,' what would your answer be?"

"I'd answer, 'Charles, it takes two to tango.'"

We had a large table at The Goring Dining Room, with luxurious five-star setting, beautifully elegant, with a panoramic view of the gardens in a landscape adorned with flowers. Benadetta looked sparklingly gorgeous, and her olive skin made me silently jealous of her beauty until I saw Bill's eyes focused on my half-exposed breasts in a low-cut, light black, silk top, a shade below my complexion. He winked at me, and I knew that was his cue of approval of the way I was dressed. Purposely, I began a no-holds-barred conversation. Why? I don't know.

"Benadetta, you look lovely." A glass of wine in my hand, I continued, "Have you ever gone to East Ham Social?" Knowing fully well that's the club she sipped the wine, gave the glass for Bill to sip, and I slapped the glass out of Bill's hand and dirtied her beautiful dress.

Charles answered. "I won't take her there. That's a place for millennials, loud music, and vulgar people. We are not of that type."

Bill concurred. "I hate to go to such a place when I'm well dressed to be among rowdy youths smoking that stink stuff."

I knew Bill wanted me to end that conversation, and he said, "Let's lift our glasses to men with beautiful wives and girlfriends who hate loud music."

Six of us lifted our glasses. Benadetta's hand went up last. She looked at me, her eyes saying, Bitch, don't f--k up the evening. You already have the man. You're going to be married to him. What's your problem? He stopped f--kin me since you came. I take him to his doctor, and I don't go in his house.

Only Charles who did not know what was taking place (or so I thought). When I looked at Bianca I could see that she was pissed. She said to the passing waiter, "I'm hungry. Bring the food. Quick."

Charles said, "I'm hungry too. I heard enough trash."

Bianca spoke. "This is lovely company. Bill is eager to address us, but not now."

"Why not now?" Charles asked.

"Charlie boy, you are the least of the apostles, so hold your question for last," Bianca said.

"Your motto is to insult me by calling me a boy before we eat," Charlie pounded the table. I did not know whether it was in jest or whether he was really annoyed by Bianca calling him boy.

"That's a term of endearment among black folks to increase our appetite when we abandon table etiquette." Bianca smiled when she replied.

I know my sister's fighting habits, so I jumped in. "Bianca, where did you buy that lovely dress?" She pretended she did not hear me. She knew I bought her dress.

She said, "Charlie, my boy, pour me a drink."

Charles poured everyone.

"I like your social ways, your etiquette, everything about you, Charles," I said.

"Who else likes my table manners?" Charles asked.

"Your wife, for sure!" Benadetta shouted.

"The Medit..." I did not know how the beginning of that word that I guarded came out of my mouth.

Bill did not let me finish the word because he knew the ending of that word. He shouted, "No! No! No! No politics. Let's eat. Let me begin my farewell speech by letting you know I'm leaving next week to go to Brooklyn to get married to the most beautiful woman in the world."

"To whom?" I shouted.

"To you," Bill shouted louder.

"Why me?"

"Because of what you do on the twin bed."

"Who else slept on that twin bed? Tell me now before we get married." I laughed when I said that.

"It isn't anybody you know." Bill coughed up his Santa ha, ha, ha.

Charles shouted. "I think I know."

Bianca shouted still louder. "Charlie boy, if you will agree to pick up the check, and tip all the people who serve our table, you are at liberty to tell us who else slept on Bill's twin bed other than Ella Willa. That's my bet. And if you lose, you will have to honor our bet and pay up like a real man."

Charles did not take the bet, and Bill stood up and addressed us.

"Ladies and gentlemen, it is so nice to have you, my friends, here tonight. Let me tell you a little of my soon-to-be sister-in-law, Bianca, who saved the day. (I knew what he meant.) Bianca came back from Brooklyn last week. She was down there for a month with her Father, who, in two weeks, will be my Father-in-law. Bianca was there to help her Father after his procedure. Bianca and I not only have the tribal smell for warfare, but she and I know her sister is cheap; and her sister considers her cheapness as being F-R-U-G-A-L. Her sister doesn't want to buy a new bridal gown from Macy's; she wants to go back to Brooklyn and dry-clean her deceased Mother's wedding gown."

"No! No! No!" everyone, except I, shouted.

Bill continued. "Friends, as you may, or may not know, my doctor said I am in the early stage of MS, but Ella Willa has given me the assurance that she doesn't say something just to say something, meaning if she says she will take care of me till death do us part, that is what she will do come hell or high water. She thinks I'm stronger than the lion that runs away from the elephant. On the twin bed, she told me I am not the wrapping paper; but I am the goods that will be wrapped, not to be exported, but to be with her for eternity. After today, I will not be making a speech, not here, nor anywhere in the world. After today, please, don't call me, except if you are calling to say you are donating five thousand pounds for Multiple Sclerosis Research.

"My future wife, do you have anything to say to these hungry people who make us spend our money in an evening with trash talk, truths, and tall tales?"

"Of course, my husband-to-be. It is so nice having the Medit...." Before I could clutch the sentence and change the word Medit, Charles rushed in.

"What's the Medit?" Charles asked. He poured himself only wine.

Bianca answered, "Charles, you won't mind if I address you as My dear Charles?" He shook his head affirmatively. "It is a place in the hood in Brooklyn that my sister and I love to hang out. Medit is loosely used as a metaphor for having good times."

A lot of whoop-de-dos went on. Our merrymaking lasted so long that we were the last to leave. But when Charles became red as a cherry in the face and spoke, we became silent.

Charles graciously lifted his wife out of her seat. I thought he was going to address me, but he addressed Bianca, in stages.

"Little-Bianca-girl, you need to polish your razzle-dazzle grammar and your virtuosity in your technique of lies and deceit as your President Trump. And here I quote an American lawman, 'Weasels and liars never hold the fields.'" He paused. "Do you want me to tell you who else slept on Bill's twin bed?"

I looked at the shock on my sister's face, prayed for her not to answer Charles, and God answered my prayer. Many times God didn't answer my prayer but that evening in The Goring Dining Room He did.

In Corinthians, believers know why they take the host and wine at communions. In the five-star London restaurant, Bianca and I, the two Americans, knew, after we ate bread and butter with our sumptuous meal, why we were outsmarted by the taciturn and uncanny Englishman, Charles.

He called the head waitress, tipped her, and said, "I know your team was already mightily tipped by the businessman who owns two dealerships in the heart of London; but this meagre tip is from me, Charlie boy, and my wife, the Mediterranean woman." He held his wife's hand, turned to his audience and said, "Bill and Ella Willa, have a wonderful wedding in Brooklyn, and stay away from the hood with its liquid, self-sacrificing metaphors."

As I listened to Charles, I felt like Pappy's hairy bitch—not Bianca who doesn't care a f--k what people say about her—shaking water off her body after I threw her to swim in the pool behind our house. It took me weeks to overcome my stupidity at the dinner table; and I learned in the interim Charles is an undercover sleuth working for the London police.

Nonetheless, I meant to invite Benadetta over for girls' talk when Bill was not at home to apologize to her for my behavior at The Goring.

17

Bill had a week without pain and stress, and I had never seen him so happy. We spent all our spare time singing duets—I on the keyboard and he with a bottle and spoon. I had taught him how to play the spoon on the bottle, musically, Trini style, with calypso music on the first and third beat. The king-sized bed upstairs had not felt the weight of our bodies for months. I did not know what gave him this renewed sexual energy, but I enjoyed his energy to the hilt on that big bed upstairs. Our romance was so new, so unique, that I began to feel our scents were tribal. And being tribal I asked him a question.

"Bill, what do you think of a black woman who hates to see a rich black man marry a white woman instead of a black woman to share his wealth with his people?"

"That's not my business. And I will never make it my business! You know such a woman?"

"I was one."

"You said was. Are you still that kind of woman like your Father?"

I did not answer. But, somehow, I did not like him comparing me with my Father.

"You don't have to answer."

I was glad when he said that.

"Ella Willa, what would you like for your wedding gift for me to remember Brooklyn and the fragrance on your body when we met?"

"I didn't know you inhaled the scent on my body that morning."

"I did."

I changed the subject because I wanted him to giggle. His giggle is so cute. "Who does it better on the twin bed—the Mediterranean or I?"

"For the past four years, I was waiting for that question. Why today?"

"Our marriage is close, and I want to know if I have a good reason to back out. I'm demanding you to tell me who is better?"

"She was good on the king-sized; you are better on any size. When I'm close to you my body does poetry and painting simultaneously. It's a feeling that I will never surrender to anyone but you. It is a fulfilling sexual relationship. With you I no longer crave for sexual gratification. When I saw you for the first time my manhood stood. Do you think your genetic brain will want your children to carry my genes? The way I felt by the old Williamsburgh Bank Building was not infatuation, a trancelike bliss, but it was a feeling of wanting you and taking you home. My spiritual GPS guided me to you. And it was for the first time in many months that I thanked God for anything; and I thanked God for meeting you, and I had prayed to Him ever since for you to marry me."

I was floored by the way he described his love for me. He was never that expressive before. I wondered if he was going to die and those were his last words before his death. I hugged him and kissed him countless times.

"Bill, Bianca will be travelling with us next week. The month she was down there taking care of Pappy, she and Judith were also making wedding arrangements unknown to Pappy."

"I want to shock Pappy."

"By doing what, Bill?" I knew he'd repeat what he said before.

"By proposing to you in front of him. I think I told you this before."

"White boy, why are you going to do that?"

"Black girl, to let him know of all the women I had in my life I've chosen you."

"I thought you only had that Mediterranean chick."

"Mind you! She has a name."

"Sorry. Mrs. Benadetta Ligo, soon I'll be Ella Willa Wilcox-Baxter."

"You'll have to drop Wilcox when we are married."

"Says who?"

"Says Mr. William Bradford Baxter, because when our zebra children grow up they will be confused as to whose last name they should use in school. Didn't that's how TV George Jefferson described the children of a black and white couple?"

"You know a lot of what takes place on American television."

We laughed the morning away. I felt so happy that my-husband-to-be is not a dud. He's jovial; he's funny; he's best in bed even in illness because he improvises. I'll be his nurse when his health fails, and will run his business. Somehow, I felt sad to know what Psalm 8:4 of the Bible says: "What is man, that thou art mindful of?" I couldn't help thinking of Bill, a man who has a successful business, who lives in a posh neighborhood in London, who views many sites from his windows, who has many cars, who, though he never told me, had countless women between his sheets. I know, because he never answered me when I questioned him about his sexual episodes.

Bianca rang. "Ella Willa, give me the information of your debit card. I want to book three tickets first class to New York. You gave me the information before but I mislaid it."

I gave it to her. "Bianca, after the wedding, how many weeks we'll be in New York?"

"You tell me."

"No more than two weeks; and I'm not going into a hotel. I want to let Pappy see me every morning preparing his and my husband's breakfast."

"What would be the Englishman and the Caribbean man's breakfast?"

"Whatever it is, they'll devour it."

"Would you be inviting Westy to have breakfast with you?"

"F--k you and him, Bianca!"

"Would you be buying a twin bed to let Pappy hear how you make noise when the Englishman is getting the goodies?"

"F--k you again, Bianca!"

"I can bring up the one in the basement so I will have an opportunity to hear if you make more noise than I make when Edward is doing the Mandingo stuff."

I laughed so loudly that Bill asked, "What was the joke, Ella Willa?"

"Bill, just sisterly days-gone-by jokes."

"I'm sure that joke was sexual; but I hope it was about me and not about Westy."

"Bill, you are a prophet."

"The English are more prophetic than the Yankees."

"Says who?"

"Says Winston Churchill."

"That English liar who jumped over a drain in South Africa and wrote in his memoir that he swam a vast span of the Indian Ocean in South Africa."

"Who told you that?"

"When my Father and Mother visited South Africa a taxi driver told them that. The taxi driver even took my parents and showed them the drain Churchill called the Indian Ocean that he said he swam over."

I kissed him, and we laughed our ass out. "Bill, if we

continue this trash talk, you would not give me time to make breakfast for you."

After breakfast I went on the keyboard and played *The More I See You, The More I love You.* He did something I never knew he could. He, too, played the song on the keyboard. I stopped, listened to him, and thought what else he knows and keeps it a secret from me. I did not tell him what I was thinking.

Benadetta called. I picked up. She said, "Don't tell Bill I called. I want to drop by and give you and Bill a wedding gift before you leave for Brooklyn."

"I hope it is not something we already have lying around."

"Like what?"

"Something as a warm spread."

"If I bring a warm spread, it will be Bill and I under it f--kin. You will be looking on, Ella Willa."

"I heard the Mediterranean woman couldn't move under Bill's gristle."

"So that's the name you call me when you and Bill smoke pot in bed?"

"You damn right!"

Benadetta and I laughed endlessly.

I forced Bill to dress, but I didn't let him know that Benadetta and Charles will be coming over. Benadetta called from the colonnade to apprise me that she's nearby. She pressed the number two button on the elevator for Bill and me, but she knew we live on the third floor. She went back down and looked for our names. Charles read the names of the inhabitants in the building and said, "They live on the third floor." He pressed the button.

The door opened on the third floor. Benadetta was casually dressed in jeans and a white T-shirt but looked so beautiful. She kissed Bill both sides of his cheek, and Charles kissed me the same way. The men hugged. But I saw when Benadetta whispered in Bill's ear, and he knew I saw her.

Bill artfully said, "Why are you two strays coming to my house at this late hour, and I didn't cook. I already gave you two hungry people a lavish dinner at The Goring. Why are you here?"

"To bring the soon-to-be-married couple a gift," Charles said.

"I hope it is not something from the thrift shop. Your wife came from Lebanon, and she's very thrifty. Did she buy the black-and-white patchwork blanket I saw in the thrift shop?" Bill asked.

"Bill, the only way my beautiful wife would bring a blanket as a gift is if she's going to sleep on the massive bed you showed me when you took me sightseeing upstairs."

I jumped in for them to end that conversation. "Benadetta, you and I will have a girls' night upstairs when I come back from Brooklyn."

She was just as eager to answer to prevent her husband from extending the bedroom talk because she spent days and nights on the massive bed upstairs. "Ella Willa, that's a deal!"

"Since that's a deal, let's drink to it. Bill, you and Charles serve the ladies. I want rum and coke. What do you want Benadetta?"

"Make it two rum and coke. Birds of a feather should flock together."

Bill rushed in. "In what sense both of you are of the same feathers?"

I said, "Tell him Benadetta."

She said, "We are both immigrants in London."

"Brexit did its job in England, and Trump will do the same in America. I like Trump. He's nationalistic." Charles looked at me.

"We the women want no politics in our house," I said.

Charles said, "I never knew this is my wife's house too."

Bill was glorious in his answer. "Let those crazy women daydream. The rum went to their soft heads. I'll put on music."

I shouted, "No canned music! I'll play." I jumped on the keyboard stool, pulled Benadetta next to me, told her to lipsink after me, and I improvised, hip hop style, as I played: "We the immigrant beauties know how to get dem limey men/ We the immigrant beauties have dem limey men beggin' for more/ Since they taste our sweetness/ From on top/ And from deep down below/ That's what dem limeys need to make dem senses grow.

Bill and Charles's voices pitched from pianissimo to fortissimo. They made their chorus and sang it four times: Give us more of the ting down below / Give us more of dat sweet ting down below/ From on top/ And from deep below/ And then one of the beauties will go on the king-sized above/ And one will go twin-sized down below.

The room became riotous. That was such a lovely evening.

Benadetta handed the gift to me and said in my ear, "Ella Willa, I love you. Bill only took me on the king-sized."

I, too, spoke in her ear. "Medit broad, we don't f--k there anymore."

"Remember he's a sick man. He has been hiding his sickness for years. I knew him long before you, Brooklyn bitch."

I looked at her, surprised myself by not saying something dirty, but smiled with a pleasant face.

"Have a safe trip to Brooklyn, and a lovely wedding. I hope one day you'll take me there to see your Pappy."

"He has a woman with Mediterranean complexion."

We hugged and laughed joyously. She showed me a belly dance movement, and I showed her the dance of a Trini woman gyrating to the ground on Labor Day in Brooklyn carnival. She laughed, and said, "That's the movement on the twin bed?"

"Yes. Benadetta, can I tell you something?"

"What, my love?"

"Would you accept my apology for slapping the glass of wine out of Bill's hand and soiling your million-dollar dress?"

"Your gentleman Bill gave me money to buy a new dress."

"Did you compensate his kindness with a nasty f--k?"

"You want to hear the truth, Ella Willa?"

"No."

"Why?"

"Benadetta, you are now my friend. And I love you. I researched your life, and I found out you were a patrician in Lebanon but the political situation there drove you to come to London. You don't like to boast, but you were an aristocrat of a noble rank from birth. I was a hand-to-mouth survivor."

She put her fingers on my lips. "You were no such thing. Ella Willa, I'm going things-for-the-kitchen shopping. What could I pick up for you when you come back a married woman?"

"Whatever is your choice, girlfriend."

"Are we still in for the threesome?"

Benadetta snatched her scarf off the rack and rushed to the elevator with her husband in pursuit. I could hear her laughter going down the elevator to the main floor.

18

We were booked first class on American Airlines to New York. I slept part of the way, but every time I got up I heard Bill telling Bianca how he missed the Concord because he would have been at JFK long ago. First class service was very good, and Bianca was in her glory when Melvy, a flight attendant, and an Erasmus High School schoolmate, gave her goodies galore. Bill eventually fell asleep, and I put a pillow below his head and covered him with my shawl.

My mind roamed to my past life, on my faith in God, and having bad luck was part of my faith in God. At times I thought God should have intervened. I kept thinking: Would Pappy like Bill? Should I have intimated Pappy in advance that Bill is a white man, even though Pappy knows. Should I remind him that Bianca had told him countless times "Love has no color." Nothing positive was coming to my mind.

My pessimism increased when I remembered what I

read of the statistics of broken marriages, especially of mixed couples. I told myself most times those broken marriages could have been prevented if they had discussed things like money, and did not listen to the naysayers. Thinking of my Father's bad ways stopped when I looked through the morning window and saw Manhattan's skyline painted in concrete, bricks, and mortars as if done by Picasso with fingers and elbows jutting here there and everywhere. But the Twin Towers were no longer two; it is one building, just as tall, just as majestic. I had dinner in the original Twin Towers with my first date after graduation from New York University and thought of returning there with him. But that never happened. He fell in love with my friend that I'd introduced him to.

The flight attendant spoke: "Buckle your seat belts, and pull your seats upright." I woke Bill, buckled his seat belt, and pushed his seat upright. I saw the big smile on Bianca's face as she hummed Home, sweet home/ Nothing's like my Brooklyn home. People were applauding as the wheels of the aircraft touched mother's earth at John F. Kennedy Airport. I applauded loudest. Bill said, "Didn't you tell me you tipped the pilot to drop us at Pappy's back door?"

"Sorry, Bill. I forgot to tip the pilot." I kissed him.

"It's the first time you didn't keep your promise."

"And that would be the last time."

"I hope I can walk when I get there."

"I will be there for you to hold."

Bianca had called Judith two days ago and told her

the exact time we will be landing, and she should take Pappy out. We wanted to surprise him, and Bill did not want Pappy to greet him when he, Bill, was pushing his walker. Judith fixed and decorated the rooms as Bianca had advised her: Bill and I in the back room, and Bianca in the middle room next to Pappy and Judith. Bianca surprised me. She prepared breakfast, and Bill ate ravenously. After breakfast Bianca and I gave Bill tales of our childhood, and Bianca annoyingly told Bill, "You see that upright piano lying with dust in the corner was Ella Willa's weapon against me to buy Pappy's love. Pappy sent me to music lessons, and I only went one day. I told Pappy I was very bad in math and to give me the money to get math lessons. In those days it was a survival game for Pappy to keep us interested in education. But in those days I was in love with Patrick, a Jamaican newcomer to Erasmus, who took my math-lessons time and money because I wanted to learn how to dance reggae just as fancy as he to show off on the girls who were also in love with Patrick. When Pappy gave me the money to pay the math teacher, I gave Ella Willa the money to double her music lessons. That's why Bianca developed her musical skills so quickly. She used my money to go for jazz lessons. It was because of my gift to her that she excels on the keyboard. Did she tell you that?"

"Yes, she did. Your big sister always says you guided her well. But, Bianca, when did Pappy know you had stopped going for math lessons because your high school grades in math never improved?" Bill asked.

"How do you know that?"

"Your sister told me."

"Bill, that's a long story. I can't tell you because Pappy may walk in any time now and hear my confession when there was a dearth of money in our house."

We heard the key in the door. Pappy's voice followed, but Judith led the way. She stopped, shifted her body, and Pappy moved forward to the sound of Good morning, Pappy. Meet my fiancé William Bradford Baxter. Before Pappy found his breath, Bill said, "Mr. James Jules Wilcox, I've come from London, England, to ask your permission, in front of you, as you requested four years ago, to take Ella Willa's hand in marriage." Bill paused. "If you agree, sir." Bill looked at me as if I had the power to tell Pappy to say yes.

I looked into Pappy's eyes, read them, and waited for his reply to Bill. Bianca looked into my eyes, and so did Judith. In that split moment my mind went back to the time when Pappy could have been imprisoned because of that white teller's lies: She said Pappy is a liar. He tried to rob the bank. Bianca and I had begged Pappy to open his bedroom door to let us in because we heard him crying. He did not. For a week neither Bianca nor I left the house. We prayed for the police not to come to arrest Pappy. Knowing Pappy's pride, we prayed that he would not commit suicide. He taught us the value of pride. Pappy was neither a helicopter parent who hovered over Bianca and me; neither was he a lawnmower parent who cleared the way of hurdles that may come our way. Pappy practiced positive parenting. He gave us reward for good behavior, and now for all his good and honest behaviors the police will soon be knocking at his door and putting handcuffs on him because of that white teller's lies. My mind went back to this lie: "I am sure I paid that black man, and now he's saying I did not pay him." The full story of the teller's lies reverberated in my brain.

I looked into Pappy's eyes and it was as if he read my mind. He shouted: "Of course, I agree, William Bradford Baxter!"

Bill held his walker firmly, knelt, and said, "Ella Willa, will you marry me?"

He opened the box with the ring. It was the first time I had seen that ring. He had taken me to Daniel Prince. A woman measured my ring finger and said, "Your fiancé is very rich." Bill was talking softly to a man, and I was asking the woman who measured my finger what is the prices of the different pieces of jewelry. She told me the prices of the hand-forged bespoke luxury jewelry and custom engagement rings that are hand-made-to-measure.

I smiled.

The woman said, "Believe me, the price means nothing to your fiancé. He'll buy it."

"How do you know?" I asked.

"I know him," she said.

After the woman measured my fingers, Bill did not take me to Daniel Prince to see the ring he bought.

My thoughts came back to Bill kneeling before me

in pain.

Quickly, I said, "Yes, yes, yes!"

I picked him up, and he put the engagement ring on my finger. Greed came to mind, and I wondered what would be the price of my wedding ring. The prices of jewelry at Daniel Prince could buy a flat in Manhattan.

Pappy said, "Judes, because of my age, I can't kneel. Will you marry me if I propose sitting on my easy chair?"

"When James Jules Wilcox? When!"

"Today." Pappy walked inside, brought back our Mother's engagement ring, and spoke in Bianca's ear. She nodded with a smile. He kissed her and said softly, "Thank you, Bianca. I'd never put your Mother's ring on another woman's finger without your consent."

Judith walked towards him. He put the ring on her finger. And we applauded.

I walked by Bianca and whispered, "Who is the star in this movie—you or Judith?"

"That's our secret." Bianca went in her room.

Pappy and Judith hugged as young lovers and went into their bedroom to do their late evening facial yoga.

The next week Judith and Bianca prepared breakfast. We chatted as a big family around the dinner table.

The piano was tuned. Somehow I believed Bianca told Judith to have the piano tuned as part of the surprise. I took the walker from Bill's hand, and walked him to the piano stool. He sat on one half of the stool, and I sat on the other half.

"What should I play, Bill?"

"*There'll be many other nights like this*/ But there'll never be another you."

I played it, and he kissed the ring on my finger.

"I'll take care of you, Bill, till the day I die."

"So you will die and leave me for the Mediterranean."

Bill and I laughed so loudly that all the parties came out of their bedrooms, laughed at us, not knowing why we were laughing.

Our double wedding, held at Antun's grounds at Queens, New York, was lovely, and blessed with close friends and family members. It was nothing like the "Jumping the Broom" wedding where the bride and bridegroom's parties were at war.

There was an erudite personality standing with a glass of champagne in his hand. Bill walked me over to him and said, "Ella Willa, meet the little boy who told me what a dealership is."

I screamed; my scream must have burst his ear drums, and my gown almost swallowed him. "Theo! Theo! Theodosius Dunkin." I hugged him. I would not let go, tears streaming down my face. "Theo, Bill speaks of you as his oxygen. He says you shaped his life; and because of you he is what he is today." I relaxed both hands around him, and he spoke.

"Did Bradford tell you what his nickname was?"

I pulled Bill in, and it was a noisy trio. Theo spoke in my ear. "No! No! He never told me. Now I know how to charm him when he is naughty to me."

Bill spoke in my ear. And I shouted, "No! No! No! Why you called Theo that?"

"Ask him," Bill said.

That meeting brought joy into my heart. Bill and I had fun with the two nicknames.

Late at night in bed Bill said, "Good night, my lovely wife."

Those words were music in my ear. "Good night, my handsome husband with that nasty nickname. Even though we did it silently in the backroom, I arrived thrice."

"What do you mean, Ella Willa?"

"When Bianca and I were children, Pappy used to tell my Mother most mornings how many times he arrived. I never knew what Pappy meant, but my little sister unraveled what arrived meant."

Bill shouted, "Oh my gawd! Oh my gawd! Pappy, I have arrived only once. What aphrodisiac you used for your many arrivals? Please, tell me, Pappy. I'm your loving son."

We laughed our way to the breakfast table.

We spent two weeks with Pappy and my joy was flowing over seeing how Bill and Pappy behaved as Father and Son teasing each other and making dirty jokes.

One morning, the household of the two married couples and Bianca were looking at *The View* on Channel 7 (ABC). There were Whoopi and her smart crew discussing a guy, a star, and his girlfriend, another star. Both stars had consensual sex, and after sex—probably satisfying—the woman told the man, "You did not pick up on my nonverbal cue."

We stopped listening to what Whoopi and her scholarly women were saying. We had our sidebars in Flatbush in a house with plenty memories, with pictures of the Wilcox family framed on every wall. Pappy was showing Bill himself wearing his first long pants at sixteen when *The View* began the discussion about the star boy and the star girl, as Pappy called them. That was a discussion Bianca reveled in more so to hear if Pappy had evolved from his prehistoric life style.

She began. "I don't know what the star girl meant by saying the star boy 'did not pick up on her nonverbal cue.' What she meant by her comment to the star boy, Pappy?" I could see the mischief in my little sister's face, pretending to be fair and nonjudgmental. But just as my little sister can make me with mud, I can make her with softer mud. And she knew that I knew what was her reason for asking Pappy that question. But she forgot that Pappy always said that he was born before his children and none of his children could outthink him. And that is what he did. He out-thought Bianca.

He got up, pulled his slackened belt around the waist of his fat pants and buttoned it tighter. He does not wear slim cut. He looked at himself sideways in the hallway mirror, then faced the mirror to measure his height and the size of his stomach. Then he stood still. He looked at Bianca and said, "Judes, let's go inside and read our Bible and leave these young people alone." Judes said, she's coming and was about to follow her husband to the bedroom when Bill spoke.

"Pappy, can you do me a favor?"

"Anything for you, my son. What's the favor you want of me?"

"Pappy, can you remain a little longer in our family discussion?"

"Sure." I could see his eyes on Bianca. And Bianca's eyes were on me saying in her mind Pappy likes Bill. He's not pretending.

"Pappy, my wife told me you almost went to prison..."

Before Bill completed his compound sentence, Pappy shouted, "Not once, twice."

"My wife only told me about the white teller at the bank who paid another black man your money because she didn't ask that other black man for his ID. And she told the bank manager with certainty that it was you, James Jules Wilcox, she paid; and that's a Federal crime for trying to rob the bank. What happened the other time when you almost went for prison?"

"I will tell you tomorrow when we have breakfast."

Judith said, "Mr. Chinaman, tell Bill about your singing talent in Fyzabad's Scouting for Talent Show."

Bill shouted: "Pappy, tell me about it! My wife told me about it, but I want to hear if from your mouth with the deep Fyzabad accent."

Pappy got up. Looked in the mirror and pulled up his fat pants and tightened his belt. He always slackens his belt before he eats. He told his audience when he reached the bridge of *Fools' Paradise* he would choke, and we should know what to do.

Bianca who was in the bathroom brushing her teeth shouted, "Pappy, wait till I'm finished brushing my teeth. I want to be there with Fyzabad's booing audience." She didn't finish brushing her teeth. She rushed out of the bathroom with her toothbrush in hand to join the Fyzabad crowd. "Pappy, go-ahead now. We know what to do."

Pappy sang beautifully, but when he reached the beginning of the bridge of the song, They say the angel I kiss/ Will fade away..., he choked. I couldn't tell if he really choked or if he played the part. But his Brooklyn-New York-Fyzabad audience shouted with bursting lungs: "Boo! Boo! Boo! Chook him down wid ah gullet. He no f--kin good." Bianca was loudest. Somehow I felt she always wanted to tell Pappy, "F--k you!" when she was in her teens and they argued about everything. So now is the time to tell him. She led the chanting, "Boo! Boo! Boo! Chook him down wid ah gullet. He no f--kin good!"

Pappy, still acting, ran off the Brooklyn-Fyzabad stage to his bedroom. His audience shouted, "Encore! Encore! Encore!" Pappy came out of his bedroom to a thunderous applause and bowed to his audience.

Judith cut up fruits; she put them on the table, and said, "Bill, I'm so happy we are in the same family now. The Wilcox family is the best."

"Judes, my gift to you is I'm paying for you and Pappy to spend your first-year anniversary in London with Ella Willa and me. Stay as long as you wish."

"Are you serious, Bill?" Judith asked.

"I'm serious as the crowd that just booed James Jules Wilcox off the stage."

Pappy got off his chair and hugged Bill. I tried to keep my eyes dry. So too was Bianca. To keep her eyes dry, she said, "Pappy, tell Bill why you evolved from hating white people. Also tell Bill what you told me why you didn't invite Virginia, your white boss, to our home for dinner." She looked at Pappy with her happy smile as when she got her first kiss from him.

I was shocked to know Pappy told me that I'm his favorite child, yet he told Bianca about his affair with a white woman and did not tell me. My mind flashed back and I remember Bianca said, boasting, "Ella Willa, you don't know Pappy as I know him because you are too close to him."

Pappy left his chair and asked me to sit on his chair because he wanted to sit next to Bill. He held Bill's hands as if he's a shaman believing the doctrine that the workings of good or evil spirits can be influenced only by the shamans, and he's one, a healer, and he's going to heal a sinner. "Bill, you are white, and no matter what white people did to black people, I love you. You are the son I never had. And when I slammed down the phone on you four years ago, before I went to bed I prayed to God to heal my hatred for white people. I think I'm healed. No. I know I'm healed. Never will I hate a white person or any person. We are all God's people."

Pappy had another question to answer: Why he

didn't invite Virginia to our home.

Bill ate many slices of mixed fruits and waited patiently for Pappy's answer. I rushed in the fridge and brought out more sliced fruits and juices. I poured Pappy half glass of pine apple juice, his favorite drink. He never drinks a full glass of anything. And he hates water with a passion. He looked at Bianca. Whenever he's in a social or cultural hot spot, he always looks at her for guidance. He never looks at me. She smiled, and that was his and her cue.

He told Bill of an affair he had with a white woman, and his wife when she was alive thought the affair with that white woman never ended. So he knew bringing Virginia, a white woman, home for dinner would be risky.

Bill asked, "Why risky? That's your boss. She invited you for dinner at her house."

"Boy [that's a Trinidad and Tobago term of endearment], I knew my wife, Enid, but as much as I thought I knew her, I didn't know what she'd do seeing Virginia, a white woman, in her house."

There was a discussion among us about infidelity, and I was shocked to hear Judith's version of infidelity.

When Pappy got up to leave the dining room, he said, "Bill, Judes and I agreed with Whoopi. If I were a woman, a man invited me for dinner, and after dinner he invited me to his apartment, and I don't want to go, I will thank him for the lovely dinner and say goodnight to him. So any woman who goes to a man's apartment after dinner goes there at her own risk."

Judith said, "Family, I want to say something. Would you allow me?"

"Sure, we want to know the effect of Chinaman after your marriage," Bill asked.

There was riotous laughter. Bill got up, and told his audience that he wants to buy some Chinamen to help his sex performance, and where he can buy it. He turned to Pappy. "Pappy, give me the address, please."

The Wilcox household was in riotous laughter until Judith stamped her foot on the floor to get our attention. And she got it.

She said, "What I want to say is political. It is our President who told over 2000 untruths before his first anniversary in office."

Pappy shouted, "They are not untruths; they are pathological lies!"

The lively family-breakfast discussion ended with kisses to each other, but Pappy's hug to Bill calling him, "My son," was touching. He and Judith went in their bedroom, and Bianca took the B41 bus to Kings Plaza mall to shop.

When Bill and I were alone, I brought my attention back to the topic on *The View*.

"Bill, don't think of us as husband and wife, but as when we were two unmarried people with heat in our pants. If I'd come to your house to get the goodies from you, and after getting your goodies and enjoying it, I write on Facebook, 'Bill, did not pick up on my nonverbal cue when we were having nice sex,' what would you tell our audience on Facebook if you disagreed with what I said?"

"Facebook nosy people, I grew up in an orphan home, and I only understand what I understand, not what other people think I should understand."

Bianca returned from shopping and saw us still discussing what was on *The View*. She said, "When I go back to London and want money from Edward, I will tell him with tears dropping on my clothes, 'You did not pick up my nonverbal cue when we had sex last night.' And when he asks me, 'What do you mean, Bianca?' I will tell him, 'I need money.'"

Bill and I laughed our way to downtown Brooklyn and renewed our vow as we touched the stone that brought us together. We shouted, "Brooklyn! Brooklyn! We come home." The owner of Halal Kitchen remembered us. He shouted, "Sister, I don't see you. Where you live now?"

I shouted back in the crowded line, "My husband and I live in London. Make it two: One for me, and one for him." Bill and I sat and ate on the same spot on the concrete edge at Atlantic Avenue where we sat four years ago.

When we returned home Pappy hugged Bill as if he were his son who returned from battle in Afghanistan. I knew when Pappy wanted to ask a question he always says, "Guess what's on my mind?" And when nobody asked Pappy what was on his mind, he chose Bill to tell him what's on his mind.

"Bill, how are you enjoying your two weeks of married life?"

"Great, Pappy."

"Do you like the way the Wilcox family treated you?"

"It couldn't be better."

"I have been living in New York for fifty years, and I am glad my deceased wife forced me to come to this country. Success was not easy to attain. Bill, how you made success you?"

"Pappy, that's a long road with a meandering story. When I left the orphan home, my friend Theo—you saw him at the wedding with Ella Willa holding on to him like if he is the life boat to save her."

"Theo is the guy with coiffed beard, Stalin's moustache, and the straight-cut English suit? Why was your wife holding on to him as if he's her lifeboat? I thought I was her lifeboat," Pappy said.

"I told Ella Willa about him, and what he taught me about life."

"What he taught you about life?"

"The first things Theodosius Dunkin told me are: running a business is not for the feint of heart; if I have six different plans, I don't have one; never undersell and over-deliver; and I cannot have a better tomorrow if I continue thinking and worrying about yesterday. He owned a funeral agency and he gave me my first job as a grave digger. He was meticulous and crazy about time. I had to be on the job one minute before his time, not a second later. I was never late because I wanted to make money. He promoted me to be his clerk, and I had to haggle with the living and the dead. People who wanted a discount because they changed their minds from burial to cremation gave me explanations that I now see why my grade school teacher told me you can do anything with numbers. A mourner told me she should get a discount because her deceased husband got two inches smaller since he's in the mortuary. She raised her voice and said she'd remove her dead. I pressed the silent buzzer, and Theo who was listening to our conversation in another room, walked in, winked at me, and said, 'Bill, give her the discount. She's correct.' When she left as the satisfied customer, Theo said that was an easy case. I couldn't believe it.

"I moonlighted in my next job as a sign painter. I was better in graffiti than anyone in the home; and I realized my graffiti skills could employ me, and it did. But back in my dead-people-living-people job, I fell in love with the organist, and she taught me the three chords I could use in playing any song and sound as a pro. I crammed those three chords in every scale, and when she couldn't be there I did her job.

"Texas was breaking out in the oil business, and I left London for Texas."

I interrupted Bill. "You never told me you lived in America."

"You are now my wife, and what I didn't tell you when we were unmarried I will tell you now."

He went back talking to Pappy. "In Texas I worked on off-shore drilling. It was hard and dangerous work, but I enjoyed it until I could no longer pollute our waters without my conscience getting sick when listening to a cacophony of complaints from people who wanted our waters to be clean.

"My only pastime was gambling. I lost my full pay, except five dollars that I hid in my shoes for transport home. Getting outside the gambling hole, I decided to save my five dollars to buy bread and milk, and walk home because I didn't have a car. A guy pulled up beside me, 'Hey, do you want to buy these winning lotto tickets?' I said, since they are winners, why not keep them for yourself? He said, 'I just realize my tank is empty, and I have to get home. You want it? Yes or no?' He dropped the tickets on the concrete. I picked it up, went into my stink sneakers, took out the five dollars, handed it to him, and he said, 'Good luck, buddy.'"

Bill stopped talking. But I learned in the four years living with him in London some of his habits. One of his habits when he wants to be dramatic is he bites his lips as if telling himself not to say a word, then he blurts out many words.

"Pappy, one of the tickets won big, and that is why success is I."

"How much, Bill?" Bianca shouted.

"My wife's adviser, I wouldn't tell you how much, and now that I'm married I have to tell my wife. But I have not forgotten how you silently took care of me when I was sick, how you drove me home from the pubs when I didn't feel well, so now you don't have to go home and tell Edward after an enjoyable sex act that he 'didn't pick up on your nonverbal cue' to hound him down for money. I have a bonus for you: After graduation you have a job with Baxter and Dunkin, and Mrs. Baxter will be your boss. The pay is good."

Bianca was speechless.

Bill continued. "My family, Theo left the funeral agency business. One day while sitting in his smelly car, he called me by my nasty nickname, he shook me terribly, and said, 'What did I tell you when we were sitting on the stoop?' 'I can't remember,' I said. He then reminded me that we should have a dealership. I shouted, 'Yes! Yes! Let's do it.' He did all the research. I trusted him with my life, and he guided me into car dealership. He runs a dealership in partnership with me. I'd never taken Ella Willa to that dealership, but she does the bookkeeping.

"Mrs. Baxter, the dealership that you run is now yours and mine. When you get back to London, my barrister will call you to sign the documents. That's my wedding gift to you, my love. Since we now have the possibility to give people things, our human capital will be investing in poverty and education all over the world."

I was more shocked than Bianca with Bill's new set of gifts to me. I walked away into the bedroom. The last thing I heard was Pappy telling Bill to take good care of me, and Bill said yes. "And my gift to you, Pappy, and your beautiful wife will be on your first anniversary I will pay your way to London, put you in a fancy hotel, with enough pounds in your pocket to treat your wife as if she's the

Queen."

"My son, are you giving me a sugar high for the moment?"

"Pappy, it is my love for you, and love has no color."

I put my both palms in my face, and I wept. Bianca came into my bedroom and held me close. "EW," that's how she calls me from childhood whenever I cry, "Pappy is now seeing the light of day." Judith, hearing our conversation, walked into the bedroom and seeing how Bianca was wiping my tears, would have no tears that time of the day.

She shouted, "Bill, you are my son too. I want to be with you, not in a hotel. Don't put me upstairs in that big, big bed."

"Why, Mother?"

"I heard from a reliable source what is done on the baby bed downstairs, and I want to experience that sexual feeling with my husband."

Bill shouted, "Oh no! Oh no! What happens in Las Vegas no longer stays in Las Vegas."

"You damn right!" Pappy said "Never trust Brooklyn women."

All the women rushed out of the bedroom, and we laughed our asses out. The men joined us and poured whiskey straight down their throats. Bill told Pappy the money he will be giving him on his first wedding anniversary is to buy bees wax to slick his hair like Nat King Cole's. That caused another round of riotous laughter till bedtime.

Our stay with Pappy and Judith was like living in a world without sin, without hatred, and without prejudice; only endless joy.

The day came for us to leave. I looked at Bill and said, "Can we stay another week, hon? Bianca's contact bought tickets for us to see *Hamilton* on Broadway."

"You have two businesses in London to attend to. No one gets successful by being away from their job."

"Yes, Bill, I understand....Bill, will you still love me if I get fat?"

"Of course. I may even borrow some of your fat. But we will have to sleep on the king-sized bed upstairs because of our weight. Would you agree to that?"

"Of course."

"Promise?"

"Promise. Honey, Uber is outside waiting to take us to JFK."

I held his hand, and walking out we heard Sonny Rollins on saxophone playing *There's No Greater Love*. Pappy always played Rollins when he was happy. We looked back and Mr. and Mrs. James Jules Wilcox were blowing kisses for us.

"Ella Willa, you forgot my walker. I need it to help me when I walk."

"Bill, when we come back it will be in the back room waiting for us. I am your walker for the rest of your life."

Instantly, I remembered our Mother told her children, "Waiting for a day to come is called patience; and when that day comes, it comes by way of your benevolence."

The day I had prayed for had come: I had the love of my Father and the love of my Husband under the same roof. Who can ask for more?

Every day I believe more in karma.

On the plane home with Bill sleeping on my shoulder, I murmured: Pappy, you, like Mother, soon your cloud will cease to be in silhouette. But when that day of your demise comes, I will never forget the love and care you have given to Bianca and me. I love you, Pappy. You told your children to dream. I had a dream, and I'm living that dream today.

I took my husband's head off of my shoulder, hugged it, kissed his thinning hair, and before falling asleep with him I thought of Pope Francis' words of advice to a married couple: "Don't put your ring on too tight; it will squeeze you. Don't put it too slack, it will fall out."

"Thank you, Pope Francis. I know you like your flock to be humble, but I'm rich now, and I'm going to have servants. Benadetta said she is going to buy things for her kitchen, and she told me that she's going to buy something for me too. But I hope my welcome gift when I get home is not an apron from that Mediterranean woman." My loud laughter awoke Bill.

"Ella Willa, where are we?"

"We are descending to the ground. Soon we will be in our home."

When I opened the door, I smiled. I reminded Bill that he promised during courtship that he would take me to see the Northern Lights on our honeymoon. "Ella Willa, our pre-honeymoon begins on the twin bed tonight."

"Honey, you are my husband, and whatever you say goes with me."

"Is that a deal, always, Brooklyn broad?"

"Always." I called his nasty name. "I love you."

"I love you too, Mrs. Ella Willa Baxter."

"Wilcox-Baxter. I'm keeping my maiden name."

We argued about the last name I should carry until we fell asleep wrapped in each other's arms.

About the Author

Lloyd Hollis Crooks is the author of *Grenada Ghost; Ice and Eyes in the Sun—True Love Comes Late, Sometimes; Peeping Through the Keyhole; Blood on the Blade,* and *Sister, Because of You...*

Crooks was a civil servant who covered "sensitive" national and international conferences in the Office of the Prime Minister in the Republic of Trinidad and Tobago during the Eric Williams Administration. To name one conference: The United States of America and The Republic of Trinidad and Tobago Leased Bases Agreement. Crooks was also a court reporter and a Parliament reporter. In New York, he was a partner's secretary in a Wall Street law firm. He lives in Brooklyn, New York, and he lectured at five CUNY colleges.